The Treasure Hunters Club

The
Secrets of the
Magical Medallions

Sean McCartney

Mason,
Thanks for
join the club!

Sean McCart

MOUNTAINLAND
publishing inc.

Secrets of the Magical Medallions: The Treasure Hunter's Club Book 1
by Sean McCartney

Production Copyright © 2010 by Mountainland Publishing, Inc.
Text Copyright © 2009 by Sean McCartney
All rights reserved

Cover Design by Todd Seipert

For information contact: Mountainland Publishing, Inc. PO Box 150891, Ogden, UT 84415

ISBN 978-0-9745476-2-6

Printed in the United States of America

To Lori, Jonah and Julia.
You are the best!

CHAPTER ONE

A Magical Medallion

Port Royal Harbor-Jamaica-1712

Maria the gypsy knew her life would end tonight. As she clenched the blue-stoned medallion an unnamed hurricane roared through Port Royal Harbor with an angry fury.

Maria repeatedly told herself she could not fail. Maria knew the danger but she had to protect the life she and others loved no matter the cost.

Rain slammed into the ground turning the streets of the small seaside town into a muddy mess. Gale force winds smashed the small homes surrounding the harbor and uprooted trees for the last three days with no end in sight.

Maria covered her face with a cloth as the rain slapped at her cheeks. She breathed deeply and staggered toward the Port Royal docks to find any vessel to get her away from this town.

The gypsy leaned into the wind as she passed the small hotel whose patrons huddled in the basement to wait out the storm. Candles flickered in a saloon's windows bright enough for Maria to see three Dorcha men watching her.

The Dorcha, followers of the dark and the enemy of the Leois, stared her down. The Leois were Maria's people.

Maria peered into driving sheets of rain. She knew evil wanted the medallion but she could not, would not, allow them to have it.

Lightning flashed across the sky and Maria saw the three men moving toward her. Water dripped off their black hats and their boots made deep imprints in the mud as they approached.

Maria turned to run, slipped, and fell face first into the muck. She scrambled to her feet, shaken but undeterred. She must keep going, she told herself.

"Going somewhere?" a cold voice asked her.

Maria didn't turn around. She looked toward the docks. Several ships in the distance heaved on the rough seas. She needed to get on one of those ships.

Maria finally faced her pursuers and did not speak. Her eyes squinted from the sting of the rain and she peered for a way out. She slipped her mud caked hand into her shawl and wrapped her fingers around the medallion. The Leois gave her this mission because of her determination and her belief in the Leois. She would justify their confidence in her by fighting until the end.

Maria began a silent prayer to the medallion trying to summon its power of light and goodness. The power did not come.

"Give me the medallion," the leader of the Dorcha said.

Maria shook her head. The Dorcha already had stolen the red-stoned medallion and Maria's mission was to get the blue-stoned medallion out of Port Royal and away from the Dorcha.

"I said I want that medallion," the man screamed and swung his open hand at Maria connecting to her cheek. She jerked back, pain exploding in her mouth as she tasted her own blood. He hit her again and this time she fell to the ground, red spit dripping from her mouth.

Maria's tear-filled eyes looked up as another burst of lightning showed her a menacing smile on the face of Evil. He held his hand out. In the other he revealed the evil medallion; its red stone glowing brightly.

"The magic is on our side," he said.

Maria breathed deeply and swung her leg with all her strength. It caught Evil's knee and he buckled to the ground, the medallion falling from his hand. The gypsy jumped to her feet and headed for the docks.

"Get her!" the man yelled to his partners. He winced in pain but straightened up, grabbed the red-stoned medallion and followed.

When Maria reached shore, every vessel was destroyed, leaving the harbor a tangled mass of splintered wood and broken planks. She heard the screams of the sailors unable to make it to shore.

"The medallion, Maria," a voice came from behind her. A chilling voice that made her skin crawl. "Let's make this as painless as possible."

Wrapping her hand around the medallion, Maria glared at the three Dorcha. A feeling of calm came over her. Though the force of the wind made her stumble, she gained strength from the medallion as she bravely stared down the followers of Evil.

Rain pelted sideways as the young woman raised her arms and began reciting a prayer.

Maria asked for freedom from danger. Behind her the sea grew angry as waves crashed into the shore with ferocity and intensity.

"This is nonsense," the leader said exasperated. "Take her."

The men went for Maria and grabbed her just as a large wave smashed into them pulling everyone out to sea.

Maria struggled in the water. She desperately grabbed a piece of wood from a shattered ship and hung on. She watched as two of the three men were engulfed in a whirlpool of water.

Waves pounded Maria as she swam toward shore. Two hands grabbed her legs and pulled her under.

Evil searched her for the medallion as Maria fought for her life. Water pressed into Maria's mouth and her lungs screamed for relief. She finally broke free and pushed herself to the violent surface.

Breaking the water Maria gasped for air.

She pulled the medallion from her pocket and stared at it. Such beauty, she thought. The ocean continued its assault as she tried to stay afloat. Maria repeated a prayer from the Leois and a peaceful calm came over her. The medallion's inner blue stone glowed as the water around her turned tranquil.

Maria saw Evil swimming toward her like a shark about to attack. She would not resist because she knew her next act was for all of humanity.

She tossed the medallion into the boiling seas just as a wave overtook her and Evil grasped at water.

The medallion skipped off the turbulent sea and sank to the bottom of the harbor.

Evil slogged to shore exhausted. Lying on his back, the rain pelting him, he reached into his pocket and pulled out the red-stoned medallion.

Lifting his weary body he attempted to go into the water to retrieve the other medallion but the sea flared up with animal rage.

Knowing the secrets of good and evil now rested at the bottom of the sea beside Maria, Evil cursed the gypsy and the violent water.

Wind and rain churned the ocean over Maria's watery grave for seven more days as white sand settled over the blue-stoned medallion.

CHAPTER TWO

A 10¢ Dream

Gunnison River-North Rim of Black Canyon, Colorado

Thirteen-year-old Tommy Reed stood in the shallow part of the Gunnison River as the water moved slowly around his boots. He used a custom-made sifter to dredge he river as he looked for his treasure.

"They are only dimes," Jackson Miller said as he cleaned water from his glasses.

"That's true," Tommy Reed said, "but can you imagine how much they must be worth now?"

"Isn't this like the old joke about the two dollar bill?" Jackson said, "You know, 'how much is a two dollar bill worth?' and the answer is 'two dollars'?"

"Paper isn't silver," Tommy said and smiled at his friend. "You could be by yourself like Chris or at home like Shannon," he said. "Besides, my Uncle Jack said this is the best place to look for the dimes."

"Then why isn't he here?" Jackson asked.

"He's in Florida with his crew working on a Spanish Galleon."

"What's the story behind these dimes anyway? Are you sure they are here?" Jackson asked.

Tommy stepped out of the river, pulled a rag from his leather satchel and dried his hands.

"In 1903 the Denver mint sent six wooden kegs of dimes by wagon trains to Phoenix. There was a bad storm and the wagons never made it. They were lost somewhere between this canyon and Montrose."

"How do you know?" Jackson asked.

"Treasure hunters found the remains of four wagons around this area and a few dimes in the river."

"So if the dimes have been found why are we here?"

"They didn't find them all," Tommy said smiling. "In fact legend has it that the bulk of the dimes were hidden from treasure hunters somewhere in the canyon."

"So you think we can find something that's been lost for over 100 years?" Jackson said.

"Are we the Treasure Hunters Club or what?"

"Most of the time it's what," Jackson said laughing.

"Just keep looking," Tommy said and bounded back into the river.

A mile up the canyon another treasure hunter, a darker more sinister man was looking for the same loot but for different reasons. He watched the teenagers dredge the river by hand.

"Young fools," he said.

One of the three men working for him approached. "Boss, why are we following a bunch of kids?"

The man didn't answer he just glared at his minion. He spit on the ground and rubbed it in with his boot.

"Keep on them and don't ever question me again."

*   *   *

Chris Henderson stood near some old oak trees and scanned the area near the water's edge. He noticed a group of small stones stacked like a pyramid against a larger boulder.

Chris stared at the formation and studied it. Looks man-made, he thought and ran toward the rocks.

On a hilltop one of the men saw Chris and pulled his walkie-talkie.

"A kid is running up the river," he said.

"Follow him," the leader replied.

*   *   *

The cell phone on Tommy's belt went off.

"Yes, Chris," Tommy said. "You're kidding," he smiled. "We are on our way." Tommy closed the phone. "He found it."

*   *   *

In minutes Tommy and Jackson worked their canoes onto a small beach area near Chris's.

Running to Chris they stopped as he stood before them holding a handful of dimes.

"Where did you find them?" Tommy asked.

"They were hidden inside a small cave surrounded by rocks. Strange thing was, when I found them, they were all in neatly stacked boxes." Chris motioned for them to follow, "You've got to see this." The group walked a bit and saw the rocks. "Move those stones and see for yourself," he said.

Tommy moved the small stones and saw stacks of cigar style boxes in neat rows.

"I don't believe this," Tommy said.

"Why?" Jackson asked.

"The dimes had to be scattered everywhere. This is the work of more than one person."

"Didn't you say some treasure hunters found some dimes by the river?" Jackson said.

"Yeah, but why hide them inside a small cave?" Tommy wondered.

Jackson thought for a minute. "Maybe a treasure hunter put them there to keep safe and forgot where he left them."

"Could be," Tommy said. "But what kind of a treasure hunter would do something like that?"

"A stupid one," a voice said.

The boys turned and saw an imposing man with lifeless eyes and a scruffy beard wearing a black, long coat and flanked by three other men.

"Who are you?" Tommy asked.

"A real treasure hunter," the man said, "not like you and your pathetic group."

"I don't think we're that bad," Chris said.

The man stared at Chris who smiled briefly then stopped. "I think I will be taking that treasure now."

"You can't do that," Tommy said.

"Who is going to stop me?"

"There are rules to treasure hunting," Tommy said.

"Which I could care less about," the treasure hunter said. "I'll bet you don't even know how much those dimes are worth."

"Um, ten cents?" Chris answered.

"Funny," he said, not laughing. "We are talking a million bucks and change."

Jackson blurted out, "More like three point two million and change," he cocked his head and said, "three million, two hundred and sixty seven thousand one hundred and sixty four…to be precise."

"So you are the smart one?"

Jackson shook his head no. He lied.

"Then shut up. This has taken up entirely too much time," the man said. He motioned to his men, "Start packing the boxes in the canoes."

"You're taking our canoes too?" Tommy said.

"Yes," he replied coldly. "Want to stop us?"

The crew of men stacked the cigar boxes into two of the three canoes.

Jackson leaned over to Tommy and whispered, "What do you want to do?"

"He is not going to take those dimes," Tommy said. "As soon as his men are done we break for the boats."

Jackson nodded to Chris who responded in kind.

"I am sure you have already thought of this, uh, sir, but with the extra weight of the dimes you are going to have a tough time navigating the canoes through the rapids," Jackson said.

"I thought you were not smart?"

"I'm not. I just think you might have some trouble."

"We can handle it," the man said.

One of Slider's men approached, "All the boxes are loaded sir."

"See now that wasn't so," the man stopped in mid-sentence as the Treasure Hunters Club sped past him, pushed the canoes into the water and started down the river.

"Get them!" the man screamed.

Chris and Tommy paddled fast with Jackson right behind them.

"Tommy," Chris said between strokes, "no matter how far ahead we get, Jackson is right, we'll never get past the rapids."

"Leave that to me," Tommy said.

Over his shoulder, Tommy saw the men get into the last canoe and push off.

"We're almost to the rapids," Chris yelled, "you got a plan?"

Tommy pulled a rope from his backpack. "When we get close to one of those old oak stumps I'm going to throw the rope around it. That should hold us, while those goons drift down river."

"What about Jackson?"

"I've got enough slack for him," Tommy said. "But I am going to need all of your strength for this one."

"No problem," Chris said.

The canoes started to bounce against the force of the water. Foam spilled into the boats.

"Any time now," Chris yelled. "The current is getting stronger."

Tommy swung the rope and threw it toward an oak stump. The rope wrapped around the stump and Tommy pulled hard.

"Hang on," Tommy yelled to Chris and flipped him part of the rope.

When the slack of the rope ran out it tightened around the stump and stopped the canoe causing it to hop on the water. Waves slammed against the boat as water flowed over the side.

"Tommy we've lost some of the boxes," Chris said his face strained.

"Tommy," Jackson yelled, "throw me the rest of the rope."

Tommy released his right hand and felt the canoe slip a bit.

"I got it," Chris said, "just get Jackson."

Tommy took the slack of the rope and threw it toward Jackson.

The young man grabbed the rope and wrapped it around his forearm and braced himself.

The water took the canoe a few feet and then it stopped. Jackson held the rope tightly, as it tore the skin from his palms. The water's speed increased and Jackson screamed in pain.

"Hang on!" Tommy yelled over the fury of the foaming river.

The crew of men got closer and reached out for Jackson's canoe but the rush of waves pushed them away.

"Paddle back to them," their leader screamed as his men fought against the rapids.

"We can't," one man said. "The water is too…" He never finished the sentence. The canoe capsized, dumping the men into the raging water.

The Treasure Hunters Club watched as the river busted the canoe to pieces. None of the men resurfaced.

"Okay, let's pull to shore," Tommy said.

"Tommy!" Jackson yelled, "The rope is not going to hold!"

Tommy looked and saw the last thread of rope snap and Jackson and his canoe drift away.

"Jump," Tommy said. "I'll throw you more rope. Just jump!"

"But the dimes?" Jackson said.

"Forget about them," Tommy yelled. "Jump!"

Jackson closed his eyes and leapt into the raging waters. The current's angry hands grabbed him just as Tommy's rope arrived, bouncing off his head.

Jackson blindly grabbed the lasso and wrapped it around his waist. Chris and Tommy pulled him into the boat.

Jackson's canoe drifted aimlessly into the rapids with the boxes of dimes falling off along the way.

"Well at least we have some of the dimes," Chris said.

"True," Tommy said. "Are you all right?"

As Jackson nodded a rush of water tore the back end of the canoe off taking the boxes of dimes with it.

"No!" Tommy shouted and lunged for the last box. But it slipped from his wet hands and he hit the floor with a thud waking himself.

Tommy's head popped up and he stared at his digital clock.

4:15 A.M.

Great, he thought, two more hours of sleep before school.

The young man lifted himself off the ground and fell back into bed. He closed his eyes and tried to sleep but he couldn't. He wanted desperately to become a treasure hunter like his famous uncle. To travel the world finding mankind's greatest treasures and…he lost his thought and shook his head.

Tommy did smile at the idea behind the dream and the many others he'd had since he and his friends formed the Treasure Hunters Club in the sixth grade.

Now two years later his club still hadn't been on any hunts and Tommy could feel them, as well as himself, getting anxious.

He pulled the covers over his head and reminded himself it was just a dream, but a voice inside keep asking when did it have a chance to become reality?

CHAPTER THREE

Diamond Jack

30 miles off Port Royal Harbor, Jamaica

The research vessel *Hanoj* moved slowly over the Caribbean excavation site. The ship's captain did not pay much attention to the calm blue water as he sat transfixed at his computer screen's magnetic sounding charts.

Diamond Jack Reed did not look forty years old or for that matter much over thirty. A man of strong convictions and the world's most sought after and famous treasure hunter, Jack's rugged good looks and his flair for drama belied his age. Treasure hunting made him extremely wealthy. His charismatic charm and zeal wooed collectors and the press.

Jack Reed won his nickname by discovering the greatest diamond mine in the history of the world. Reed led an expedition into the deep jungles of the Congo to find another Hope Diamond, the most famous blue diamond ever.

With his unbelievable luck, Jack stumbled on an entire mine of blue diamonds. Though the Congo government denied excavation access to an American, the publicity Jack received catapulted him into the world of fame and money.

Using his newfound success Diamond Jack assembled a team, his "crew" he called them, and went on the hunt for more treasure.

Reed's incredible luck continued as he and his crew found a treasure off the coast of Oyster Bay, New York believed to belong to the pirate Captain Kidd. The treasure's estimated worth was thirty million dollars.

Other treasure hunters cursed Reed's magic touch and cringed when Diamond Jack Reed and his crew made yet another of the greatest discoveries of the twentieth century. Searching in West Central Mexico, Reed uncovered gold and jewels belonging to the Aztec Empire. Treasure hunters had been looking for these artifacts for centuries but it required a man like Diamond Jack to find them.

With his reputation, Reed could afford to pick and choose his hunts. When he found rare coins that to him did not have much value, he sent them to his nephew, Tommy Reed.

Without a wife and not really wanting one, Jack liked to think of Tommy as his own son. He didn't get along with Tommy's dad, but that did not stop Jack from enjoying a good relationship with his nephew.

As he looked at grid charts in the *Hanoj* control room Diamond Jack Reed knew this current treasure hunt could be his last if he and his crew came through for their wealthy employer. The money generated would make them all rich beyond their wildest dreams.

Then maybe he would settle down and take life easy? Maybe Elizabeth, Jack wondered, could be the person to do that with?

Elizabeth Haden worked with Jack for over ten years. She began as a starry eyed dreamer when she first met Jack and blossomed into one of the best treasure hunters on the crew.

Jack liked having her around as she brought a woman's thoughts and ideas to the tasks before them. Though Elizabeth Haden once told Jack Reed he could be no one's husband, she shared his passion for treasure hunting.

"How does it look?" Elizabeth asked as she came into the boat's navigation space.

"Hang on," Jack said. He spoke into a small microphone that was hooked up to a radio. "Have you got one, Shawn?"

"Yes, sir," Shawn's voice crackled over the speaker. "Got a hit at forty degrees off the starboard side."

"Roger that," Jack said and used a pencil to mark on his grid paper.

Jack stared at his computer screen. Charts and maps lay on top of one another on his desk.

"What?" Jack finally asked Elizabeth.

"The magnetic survey," Elizabeth said. "Have we been able to narrow our search?"

"Yes," Reed said. "Shawn's done a great job and has found a major magnetic anomaly in this section of the water."

"Is it part of a larger wreck?" Elizabeth asked.

"Doesn't matter," Reed said. "What we are looking for is not going to be on a ship; it is going to be on the ocean floor."

"Jack," Elizabeth began, "the guys and I think it's time you told us exactly what are we looking for? You've never kept it a secret from us before this hunt."

Jack paused. "A special medallion."

"A medallion?"

"Yes."

"We are looking for a medallion from what time period?"

"Around the eighteenth century."

"You've got to be kidding." Elizabeth started to laugh. "Between the ocean currents, hurricanes and everything else that goes on in these waters, you're telling me we've been out here for over a year looking for a needle in a haystack?"

"Have you lost faith, Elizabeth?"

"No," she stammered, "it's not that. But come on, Jack, you know how difficult finding such a small piece is going to be."

"I do," Reed acknowledged. "But I also know that I have found treasures others said were impossible or did not exist. Shawn's work on the magnetic survey and the work from the others on the mag vessel are making things easier. Besides, if we do this right the site will make me super rich and I can retire." He pulled another map over the ones lying on the desk and took out a pen. "You probably can to."

"What?"

"Retire when we find this medallion."

"I'm too young to retire," she said proudly.

"No one is too young to retire," Jack said.

"Why is this piece so important?"

"I am not sure. Our employer desperately wants it. I figured by making my fee ridiculous he'd give up, but he said it was no problem and I was on board. Truthfully, I have seen so many different medallions come off these sea floors that I find it hard to differentiate between any of them."

"So what is special about this one?"

"Supposed to be made of gold and have some sort of blue stone in the middle of it."

"With over three hundred years of salt water that stone might not be there anymore."

"I told our guy that, but he didn't seem to mind."

"What's his name? Is he a collector?"

"Manuel de la Ernesto and he might be a collector," Reed shrugged. "I didn't ask."

A young man entered the control room wearing a scuba diving outfit.

"Jack, we are ready to dredge the area."

Reed nodded. "Good. Make sure the pumps are all right and you and Shawn can go down."

"Will do," the man said and was gone.

"Were you able to fix the water fed dredges?" Elizabeth asked forgetting about her and Jack's discussion.

"Yeah," Jack said, "took a bit of doing but we managed."

"So you're using both pumps?" Elizabeth asked.

"For what we are being paid I would vacuum the floor of the Atlantic Ocean if I had to," Jack said with a smile.

Elizabeth frowned and looked at Jack strangely. "It isn't just for the money, is it Jack?"

Reed stopped looking at his charts and turned to his most prized pupil. His blue eyes beamed. "No, it's always about the chase; solving the puzzle. And if we can make some money in the process then so much the better."

He hoped his lie got by her. He didn't like to talk about what he felt and though he could imagine the end of his career, he didn't want to admit it to anyone.

Elizabeth smiled in relief. "Good," she said. "I'll go help the rest of the crew."

Diamond Jack Reed returned to his charts but in the back of his mind he was thinking about retiring in comfort. The thrill that kept him on the chase for so many years had faded for the hunter and now he had to look harder for inspiration.

As he stared at the maps, maybe, he feared, neither inspiration nor the medallion was out there anymore.

CHAPTER FOUR

The Treasure Hunters Club

Tommy Reed ran his hand through his dark hair as he walked the aisles of the Mythological Artifacts Exhibit in awe. As a founding member of the Treasure Hunters Club, he made sure he never missed a chance to see real world treasures even if the artifacts were replicas.

"Tommy, the weapons are over here," his friend and fellow treasure club member Chris Henderson said.

Tommy walked to the weapons exhibit and smiled with great satisfaction. The Mythological Artifacts Exhibit displayed the history of legendary treasure, along with information cards describing all the interesting facts of each item. The mythical originals of these fakes, Tommy thought, were once the object of every treasure hunter in the world based on only the rumor they might exist.

Tommy stared at a nineteenth century chief's ax which was a long stick with a rock tied to it belonged to the Oceanic God of the forests. There was an iron sword from Denmark used by the Norse God Frey that had the ability to fight on its own. In a large glass case was a bow with two arrows used by Diana, the Roman goddess of hunting. Hanging up was a suit of armor designed by Hephaistos for Achilles, the great Greek warrior, to protect him when he went to war in Troy.

A few feet away, in a special sealed off area, was a weapon of great distinction.

"Chris, look at this," Tommy pointed at the large case. "Thor's hammer," Tommy said staring at the mighty object.

The Norse god Thor's hammer, called the *mjollnir*, never missed its target and always returned to Thor's hand whenever he threw it.

"It's fake," Chris said unimpressed.

"So?" Tommy said. "I'll bet there were centuries of treasure hunters who looked for Thor's hammer."

Chris walked to another part of the exhibit while Tommy read every information card, some twice.

"What are these?" Chris asked as he pointed at two brass objects suspended in the air.

"Those are *vajras*," Tommy said. "Seventeenth century from Tibet, sometimes called the 'Thunderbolt Scepter.' Hindu gods Indra and Karttikeya used them as weapons."

"They threw them?"

"I guess," Tommy shrugged. "The Tibetans believed that those thunderbolts held magical powers to destroy evil forces."

"Do they?"

Tommy glanced at Chris and said, "They're fake remember."

"Oh, yeah," Chris said.

Tommy and Chris continued through the exhibit when they came across a table of medallions resting on a sheet of blue velvet. Tommy looked at the small cards next to each medallion. Before he could read any of them he was interrupted.

A large man in a blue blazer with the Civic Center logo on his lapel announced, "The exhibit will be closing in ten minutes but the gift store will remain open for another hour."

"Come on," Chris said, "we've got a meeting."

Tommy took one last look around and decided he would come back to the exhibit when he had more time to study and read everything. He followed Chris outside to the bike rack.

"Can't wait to tell the others what we saw," Tommy said as he unlocked the chain holding his bike.

"You know Jackson will love the weapons," Chris said.

"And Shannon?" Tommy said pushing on a pedal.

"She's a girl," Chris said and got on his bike, "God only knows her reaction."

The Treasure Hunters Club met "officially" once a week but most often everyday depending on what the group wanted to talk about.

Their clubhouse, an old trailer home, sat in the backyard behind Tommy's house and from the outside looked abandoned and rusted, until you went inside.

Tommy slid his coded key card through the lock and the green light gave him permission to open the door. When he walked in Shannon and Jackson were already seated at a small, round oak table.

"You're late," Shannon barked as she threw a book on top of a bookshelf which stored many historical and archeological readings.

"We got held up at the exhibit," Tommy said smiling.

"You got stuck looking at all the weapons, didn't you?"

Tommy tried to avoid eye contact, but with Shannon it proved too difficult.

The two lived on the same street since birth and had been friends since they could walk. Tommy only recently noticed how pretty Shannon's brown eyes were next to her sandy blond hair.

"I like the weapons," Tommy said as he took a seat.

"What did you see?" Jackson asked enthusiastically.

Jackson Miller was, without a doubt, the smartest of the group. He tested out of every math level the middle school offered and was taking advanced placement math at the new high school. For Jackson the AP, advanced placement, classes offered a challenge. And the one thing the young African-American man enjoyed more than anything was an academic challenge. However, when it came to common sense of humor, Jackson fell behind. The group always joked with him about being the boy with two last names. It took him a while to realize they were kidding and to see that in fact he did have two last names.

"Next time you can come with us," Tommy said to Jackson.

"Can we start?" Shannon asked.

"Yes," Tommy said and stood at the front of the table. "I call this meeting of the Treasure Hunters Club to order. All the members please say aye if present."

Three "ayes" sounded loud and clear.

"Then we shall begin," Tommy said. "I would like to discuss mystery behind the lost treasure of Harry Morgan. In 1671 after his buccaneers beat the Spanish in Panama he supposedly hid the main part of the treasure from his men." Tommy noticed everyone starting to drift off.

"Is this boring you guys?" he said.

"Huh?" Chris said breaking from his trance.

"Come on guys pay attention," Tommy said.

They all apologized but Tommy understood their feelings. Talking about treasure hunting did not seem as exciting anymore.

"Speaking of Harry Morgan how many ships have been lost in the Caribbean?" Jackson asked.

"Hundreds," Chris said, "maybe thousands."

"And how many had loot on them?"

"Depends on if they were a pirate ship or a Spanish galleon," Chris said.

"I read that Spain was able to get most of the gold away before Morgan could get to it. Besides, it wasn't like the pirates kept good records or anything," Tommy said. "They were thieves and robbers."

"Like Captain Kidd?" Shannon said.

Tommy looked at her and shook his head.

"I'm just kidding, Tommy. We can't all be like your uncle."

"By the way, where is he right now?" Chris asked.

"Last e-mail he sent told me he was going to Jamaica for an excavation."

"You know where?" Jackson said and went over to a computer, "maybe we can find him?"

"He'll send an e-mail," Tommy said.

"I wish we could do what he does," Shannon sighed.

"So do I," Tommy said.

There was silence until Shannon said, "Why don't we."

"Don't we what?" Chris asked.

"Set up a treasure hunt for ourselves."

"Where?" Tommy asked.

"Some place in the Caribbean."

"That's realistic," Chris said shaking his head.

"Why not?" Shannon said feeling offended. "You think we can't do it?"

"We can do the research part, Shannon," Chris said irritated, "but we can't go on a real hunt because we have no money."

Tommy nodded, "He's right. My uncle gets a lot of money to do these digs. Especially since he is the best in the world."

A knock at the door startled the club.

"Who is it?" Tommy yelled.

"Your dad," came a gruff reply. "Time for dinner," he said, "and your friends can't stay."

Jackson peeked out the window and saw Tommy's dad walk slowly back to the house. The math whiz turned to Tommy and said, "Tommy, I don't get...,"

"I know," Tommy nodded. "How can Uncle Jack, an adventurer and explorer, and a stiff come from the same mother? I ask myself that often."

"It's not his fault," Shannon said. "A lot of people are down after losing their jobs with this economy."

"He could be nicer," Tommy said.

"We are outta here," Chris said as the others followed him waving goodbye.

Shannon stuck her head back through the door.

"He's not that bad, Tommy," she said. "Everyone can't be as great as your Uncle Jack."

"I know," Tommy said smiling. "I'll see you in school."

When the door shut Tommy turned off the old computer. He made sure all the doors and windows were locked. As he made his way out the door he glanced at the World and United States maps on the wall. The group put colored pins in all the places Tommy's uncle found treasure. There were so many, Tommy thought.

Just before he opened the door he looked at the almost empty treasure case with its many empty shelves. There were a few things Uncle Jack had sent Tommy but nothing the group found. Tommy frowned as he thought of all the talk of filling the shelves with treasure. That's all it is, Tommy figured, just talk.

Tommy closed the clubhouse door and sulked into, as he often said, the house where dreams went to die. He would endure another dinner with his dad scowling and his mother cowering in fear. Why couldn't they get themselves together? he wondered. Just pull yourself up and start something new. Never let anything stand in the way of what you want. That's what his Uncle Jack always told him.

Tommy sat at the table and breathed slowly and deliberately. His mom, cigarette dangling from her lips and eyes swollen from crying, spooned potatoes then corn onto his plate before slicing off a piece of meatloaf.

Tommy's dad sucked down another beer and shot angry looks at Tommy and his wife. All that hate, Tommy wondered, where did it come from? More importantly why was it directed at him and his mother?

The young man sat in silence and ate as he waited for the nightly explosion of anger that always accompanied a Reed family dinner.

CHAPTER FIVE

Money Man

Jack and Elizabeth sat in a secluded table near the back of the restaurant and waited for Manuel to arrive. Rain drove most of the patio diners inside, though two younger couples stayed outdoors drinking Sangria and getting soaked. The restaurant specialty was jerk chicken and fried potatoes, a dish Jack Reed started to call his favorite after over a year of work.

"How old is Mr. Ernesto?" Elizabeth asked.

"Don't know," Jack replied looking at the doorway.

"He's from where? Spain?"

"Never asked."

"You never asked?"

"No, it never came up."

"I've got to say that I have never heard of a famous Ernesto family. What are they, like royalty of Europe or South America?"

"I don't know," Jack shrugged.

The waiter came to the table.

"Two Tings please," Jack said and turned his attention back to Elizabeth. "He pays us a lot of money."

"Is that all you are worrying about?"

"Liz, I would love to tell you that we are searching for something that is going to help mankind understand history better, but unfortunately we are doing this for a ton of cash."

"I'm surprised at you, Jack," Elizabeth smiled at the waiter as he put two bottles of Ting, Jamaica's own grapefruit soda on the table.

"Why?" Jack said surprised.

"Because when I first started you told me that treasure hunting was meant to clarify, understand and, in a way, touch history."

"You also have to live, my dear. When it's this much money, we'll clarify history later." Jack's eyes looked up. "There he is." Jack waved his arm to the new diner.

Elizabeth turned to see an elderly gentleman with a tan shirt and matching pants. He used a handkerchief to wipe the rain, or was it sweat, Elizabeth wondered, from his brow. He looked like a young-looking grandfather, but something about him did not sit well with Elizabeth.

"Be nice," Jack said and stood up. "Manuel, over here."

Manuel de la Ernesto walked to the table followed by two large men with no necks and large bodies.

"Jack, so good to see you again," Manuel said pulling a chair from the table.

"Manuel, this is my top assistant Elizabeth Haden."

Manuel smiled at her before sitting down. "Such beauty." He grabbed her hand and kissed it gently.

"Charming," Elizabeth said unimpressed.

"What can I get you?" Jack asked.

"Tequila will be fine."

Jack motioned to the waiter.

"Do they need anything?" Jack asked referring to the other men.

"They are fine."

"You must be pretty important to have two bodyguards," Elizabeth said.

Manuel waved the woman off with a smile.

"Now, Jack, tell me how it's going and what my money is buying me."

"We had a good week," Jack began and took a sip of his drink. "We dredged over two miles of grid area and hauled in a ton of stuff."

"Jack, I have spent a lot of money to get this medallion back into my family."

"I know, and you have been very generous with this expedition. But you must understand we are not looking for something large like a ship or a treasure chest. You want a small medallion that was lost over three hundred years ago. It's going to take time."

"But you are the best," Manuel said and slammed back his tequila drink. "Or are you not the Diamond Jack I have read so much about?"

Jack gave a weak smile and bowed his head before speaking. "No, I am the same and I am sure when we are done with our reverse electro dialysis we will surely turn up something."

"I am sorry for my ignorance but what is reverse electro dialysis?"

"A way to clean the artifacts," Jack said. "But with the medallion being made of gold, as you have said, then it will not be harmed."

"Why?"

"Because gold can last," Jack said, "even on the ocean floor for centuries."

Manuel looked at Jack strangely, "But what of the gem in the middle?"

"That's why it will need cleaning."

"And how long does this reverse thing take?"

"Depends on the size of the artifact; how old it is; how much debris is on it."

Elizabeth waited for a lull in the conversation as Manuel thought about Jack's answers and spoke, "Mr. Ernesto, why is this artifact so important to your family?"

A cell phone rang and Manuel pulled the slender object from his pocket. "Yes," he said and listened, his expression never changing. He held his hand to the phone and said, "I must take this. Please excuse me."

Manuel got up from the table and walked to the front door talking quietly into his phone, his two bodyguards following.

Jack smiled as Elizabeth frowned.

"What?" he asked.

"Jack," she shook her head, "you trust this guy?"

"I don't need to trust him as long as his checks clear. He doesn't even know what type of medallion he's looking for."

"Do you?"

"Doesn't matter. We'll give him a medallion when we find one, cash his check and retire."

"There is something strange about this guy. I mean, he's got those two huge monsters that follow him and he never answers a question straight. Don't you see that?"

"No, I don't," Jack said.

"All right then," Elizabeth said.

Manuel walked back to the table smiling. "Business never takes time off."

"Mr. Ernesto," Elizabeth began.

"Please call me Manuel," he said.

"Manuel," Elizabeth said smiling, "we were interrupted by your call but I was wondering what is so special about this medallion? I mean you've spent a lot of money. Is it really worth that much?"

"I have collected jewels and artifacts from all over the globe that once belonged to my family. I am the last of the Ernesto clan and I want to keep my name and my heritage alive," he said and reached into his pocket. "Look at this," he said and held a medallion close to Elizabeth. It was the size of his hand with a red stone in the middle. "I had this recovered from the Straits of Florida and through exhausting research found that another medallion of this exact size, only with a blue stone, is out there."

"So?"

"Many people believe that medallions have, how would you say, magical powers, Ms. Haden."

"That's why you want these medallions? For magic?"

Manuel laughed, "Of course not. Their value separately is worth nothing. But together," he shook his head, "then their worth would rise considerably."

Elizabeth looked at Jack, "So it is all about the money."

"No, my dear," Manuel said. "This one," he held up the medallion, "is something special to the Ernesto family and I will not feel good until I have the other one for the collection. When I am gone I will donate all of my treasures to museums and the family name will live on forever."

Elizabeth said, "Where is your family from?"

"All over really," Manuel said. "Classic nomads, the Ernestos. We have settled in many places."

"Where exactly?" Elizabeth pressed.

Manuel smiled and ignored the question and turned to Jack. "When you have something, Jack, please call."

"I will."

Manuel rose from the table and bowed to Elizabeth. "Ms. Haden, your beauty is only

matched by your intelligence."

Elizabeth smiled still unimpressed and said, "You are too kind."

"The dinner is on me," Manuel said and walked away.

"What will you have?" Jack asked a quiet Elizabeth.

Elizabeth watched Manuel leave with his hulking bodyguards and said, "I don't care what you say but there is more to this Ernesto family than he is telling us. Did you see the way he avoided the question about his family origins?"

"Some people are just private. I wouldn't share my family's sad history," Jack said.

Elizabeth didn't seem satisfied. "No medallion is worth that much and his talk about magical powers was creepy," she said.

"Well until you find out something different I say we enjoy the meal on our employer and have some more of this grapefruit soda."

"So you don't mind if I do some checking around?"

"Do your best."

"I plan to," Elizabeth said, her mind already working.

CHAPTER SIX

At School

Kennedy Middle School sat on the eastern part of town with over eight hundred students, grades six through eight. Kennedy paired with another middle school on the west side of town to funnel students into an already crowded, newly built high school.

As an eighth grader, Tommy Reed felt an incredible urge to move on to the high school. Tommy hung out with his friends in the Treasure Hunters Club and usually got good grades and did his best to stay out of trouble.

Tommy never considered himself the most popular kid at Kennedy. He fit into the niche of the quiet ones who worked for good grades. His friends, with the exception of Jackson who was super smart, were just like Tommy. Teachers never worried about them turning in assignments because they always did.

"It's not that hard," Shannon would say.

While grades never worried Tommy, walking the hallways during class changes did. A student named Zachary Butler terrified Tommy and many others.

Zach was the class bully with a large body, thick hair, dark eyes and a bad attitude. He'd repeated the eighth grade so many times there was a rumor he had his own parking space in the teacher's lot. Like a shark sensing a wounded fish Butler zeroed in on Tommy during the switch to Language Arts.

"Tommy," Zach said as he grabbed Tommy by the back of the shirt.

Tommy felt his heart leap. "Yeah, Zach," Tommy said as he turned to the man child.

"I didn't bring my lunch today."

"That's too bad."

"I was thinking you could help me with that."

"How?"

"By giving me yours."

Tommy smiled, "I didn't pack a lunch. I'm buying the school lunch."

"That's good because I can just take your money then."

"You're taking my lunch money?" Tommy said aghast. "Isn't that a little cliché? I mean, Zach, it's the twenty-first century. You can't think of anything better than taking someone's lunch money?"

Zach thought for a moment, clearly stuck on the word cliché and finally said, "I could just start punching you in the face."

Tommy's eyebrows raised, "Okay, not really what I had in mind."

"Then give me what I asked for," Zach said and pulled Tommy close to him.

"Hey, what's the problem?"

Tommy looked up to see Shannon.

"Zach, what are you doing? Let him go," she said, "or you and I are going to have a problem."

Zach released Tommy from his grasp and stared at Shannon.

Tommy straightened his shirt and whispered, "Thank you," to Shannon and walked away.

"No problem," Shannon said quite proudly and turned to Zach. "Stop giving me your tough guy stare. I don't buy it. But if you're feeling froggy go ahead and jump. I smacked you down before and I don't mind doing it again."

Zach didn't move. For all his bravado Zachary Butler could not deal with Shannon McDougal. When they were younger she would routinely beat him up for picking on smaller kids. When she wasn't around, Zach could dominate a room, but if she was, he'd slink into a corner and not come out. For this and many other reasons Tommy Reed enjoyed having Shannon in the Treasure Hunters Club.

*   *   *

As the end of the day neared, Tommy walked into his final class, Mr. Crist's Social Studies. His favorite. Tommy learned from his Uncle Jack the value of history and always enjoyed the lessons, even if some of his classmates did not.

He saw the video set-up and wondered what selection Mr. Crist pulled from his ever expansive collection of DVDs.

Again, like most teenagers, the dark lights and soft, documentary voice at the end of the day just lulled Tommy into a stupor. Unfortunately for Tommy and the rest of the class, Mr. Crist handed out a question sheet that went along with the movie. And of course it was for a grade.

The movie came from a History Channel program called "History's Mysteries" and contained stories about lost ships and their treasures.

Though interested in the topic, after the first twenty minutes Tommy felt his eyes droop and his head tilt around. He couldn't stay awake. He tried to refocus on the movie but his eyes became too heavy. Finally he shook his head and blinked several times and that's when the narrator caught his attention.

"In 1712 one of the worst, most violent hurricanes swept through the Port Royal Harbor in Jamaica destroying over thirty-eight ships that were believed to be carrying millions of dollars of coins, jewelry and silver."

The narrator continued but Tommy drifted off again. His mind wondered to a recent e-mail from his Uncle Jack. He was in Port Royal, Tommy remembered. He hoped Uncle Jack would send him something from his excavation.

Tommy closed his eyes and pictured himself on a ship discovering buried treasure, his friends right by his side. The dream reoccurred often and Tommy longed for the day when he would be a real treasure hunter.

Tommy watched the final moments of the video as it showed the devastating effects of a hurricane on wooden ships. He cringed at the destruction.

As the video ended Tommy wrote his name on the question sheet and turned it in to Mr. Crist.

Tommy kept his dream alive that someday he would be out on the seas just like his uncle, finding lost treasure and gaining fame for every discovery.

*   *   *

The busses spewed smoke and waited in the bus port at the back of the school building as the students of Kennedy came pouring out. The administration staggered the dismissal times so the younger students could get to the busses first.

A seat on the bus wasn't a problem for Tommy. The problem, from his view, was avoiding Zach Butler. Twice during the year the oversized eighth grader caused Tommy to miss his bus. Once while sitting on him and one time Zach stole Tommy's book bag, which Shannon got back immediately but it didn't make Tommy feel any safer.

Tommy wanted to blend in with a crowd and avoid Butler completely.

Mr. Crist dismissed the class and Tommy sprinted to his locker, grabbed his books and quickly got to the stairs. He started down and stopped.

Zach stood at the bottom of stairs looking like a lion ready to pounce. Tommy turned around and started back up the stairs when Chris and Jackson appeared.

"Let's go," Jackson said smiling.

"Wrong way, dude," Chris said.

"Look," Tommy pointed to the bottom of the steps.

The boys didn't move.

"Shannon is at gymnastics," Jackson said.

"We don't need her," Chris said confidently.

"Yes we do," Tommy said.

After a long pause Chris finally said, "Screw this. I'm going."

Watching their friend's courage did little to help Jackson and Tommy feel up to the task but they followed anyway.

A pack of seventh grade girls started down the steps at the same time and the boys fell in line with them. They passed Zach when his voice rang out, "Reed, I'm coming after you!"

Tommy slammed into one of the girls and they both fell to the ground. Her scream caused the other girls to squeal and laugh but it did not stop Zach's pursuit.

Chris and Jackson stepped in front of the massive boy and Zach bowled them over.

Jackson looked at Chris and said, "I thought you had him?"

"I thought you did," Chris said.

"Forget it now because he's about to kill Tommy."

Tommy scrambled to his feet and ran toward the door. All he had to do was make it through and his bus was waiting outside. Five steps away, he told himself, and then he saw Zach step in front of the door, arms crossed and legs spread with a look of "gotcha."

Without thinking Tommy continued running at the building-sized boy and at the last second slid, like a baseball player coming into home, under Zach's legs and out the door.

Butler turned around just as Tommy stepped onto his bus. Chris and Jackson went through a different door and joined Tommy.

The bus pulled away and the three boys watched as Zach Butler stomped in anger at missing his prey.

Tommy looked at his friends and breathed a sigh of relief. "We need a plan for dealing with him," he said, "because someday either he's going to get us or we are going to have to get him."

"He's bound to get in trouble," Chris said.

"Chris is right," Jackson agreed. "I mean the kid is what thirty? Thirty-one?"

"Maybe we could get him on child abuse charges or endangering a minor?" Tommy said laughing.

"That is definitely our next step," Chris said.

CHAPTER SEVEN

Discovery

Eric Stone helped Shawn Dawkins, one of Jack's top crewmen clean the artifacts from the dredge by placing them into large water tanks.

"What's next?" Eric asked.

Stone recently joined the crew while they were in Jamaica. Though he was young, his work ethic impressed the others as he learned the ropes of working an excavation site.

"We start the reverse electro dialysis," Shawn said.

"Wouldn't a pick ax or acid work faster?"

Shawn laughed, "If we want the artifacts destroyed we'll use your method. Mel Fisher developed reverse electro dialysis for the specific purpose of cleaning ancient artifacts. See the process separates oxygen molecules from the Fe_2O_3 deposits which have caked on the sunken relics.

"When artifacts are excavated from the bottom of the ocean they are encrusted with coral concretion. Organisms attach themselves to the artifact then die, leaving skeletal remains as hard as concrete. Conservation is the process of stabilizing and protecting artifacts from further deterioration using specific treatments. The goal is to preserve the artifact."

"How long will this take?" Eric asked.

"The treatment process can take a few hours or a few years depending on the material. The stuff we are looking for shouldn't take long at all."

Eric stared into the large tanks. "Wow, look at all of this stuff. Looks disgusting with all the residue coming off of them."

"We've got to make sure to keep the artifacts wet because if they are exposed to air before the treatment is complete, the artifact will alter its physical and chemical state."

"What year are those coins from?" Eric asked.

"Probably the eighteenth century and stolen by pirates," Shawn said.

It took the two men a while but Dawkins pulled six medallions from the cleaning. Two were perfectly intact while the other four were chipped and broken.

"That's what we are looking for," Shawn said holding the medallions in his hand. "Call Jack."

"These don't look very good," Eric said.

"I'll clean up the ones that are salvageable and the rest we'll throw away."

Eric made the call to Reed.

"He's coming," Eric said and watched Shawn begin the cleaning process. "I thought there was only supposed to be one medallion."

"When it comes to excavating," Shawn said, "you never know what you are going to get."

*   *   *

Tommy walked slowly up the steps to his front door. His backpack hung off his right shoulder and he set it down in the doorway without a sound.

When he entered the house his father snored loudly on the couch and his mother was in the kitchen sniffling over a mixing bowl as she used a spoon to stir something.

"Hey, Mom," Tommy whispered, careful not to say anything to wake his dad.

His mom smiled weakly and said, "Hi, honey, how was your day?"

"Good," Tommy said. "Mom, are you okay?"

"Sure," she said as the tear stains on her cheeks cracked. "Everything is great."

Tommy felt helpless. He wanted to comfort her but didn't know how he could. He wondered how his family seemed to go so far off track.

"I'll be out in the clubhouse," he said.

His mom nodded and said, "Fine."

Before he went out the backdoor he asked, "Are you sure you're going to be all right?"

His mom breathed deeply and said, "Yeah." They both shuddered when they heard the snorer move. "Yeah," she reiterated, "I'll be fine. You go."

*   *   *

Jack arrived in the conservation room very excited with Elizabeth in tow.

"Where is it?" he asked.

"Actually, Skip, there were six medallions. Four were worthless, all smashed up, but two of them are intact and look pretty good," Dawkins said.

"Two?" Jack responded.

"Yeah."

"What did you do with the other four?" Elizabeth asked.

Shawn pulled out a plastic bin and showed them the broken medallions. They all agreed they were not worth keeping.

"Which one has a blue stone in the middle?" Jack asked.

"Both do."

"Let me see that," Jack insisted and looked at each medallion, turning them over in his hands for several seconds before handing them back to Shawn.

"Well?" Elizabeth asked.

"Well what?" the famous treasure hunter said.

"Do you know which one of them he wants?"

"I'm thinking the one with the Spanish markings, since Manuel is Spanish."

"Claims to be," Elizabeth said. "You know Jack through all of my research the name Ernesto doesn't come up at all. I don't think he is who he says he is."

"His checks clear," Jack said with a smile and a wink.

Exasperated Elizabeth said, "All right then where are the other markings from?"

"Don't know," Jack said. "They are unlike anything I have ever seen before and I've seen a lot."

Elizabeth grabbed the medallions and looked at both. She carefully studied the medallion with the strange markings.

"Seems like a form of hieroglyphics, but these markings don't look like pictures, more like symbols. Are you thinking eighteenth century?" she asked.

"Maybe," Jack said. "Shawn, run this through the computer. Then we can make a definite choice."

Jack studied the medallion with the unusual markings more closely. "I don't think this is the one and if it isn't I'm going to send this to Tommy. I haven't sent him anything good lately."

"That's your brother's kid?" Shawn asked.

"Yeah," Jack said with a smile, "great kid but a lousy home life. Here, take these to the lab and see what you can find out."

"No problem," Shawn said and left.

Jack shook his head, "I never could understand my brother."

"Wouldn't he say the same thing about you?" Elizabeth asked.

Jack thought for a moment and said, "Probably."

"I don't get it," Elizabeth said, "what is it that you two can't stand about each other?"

Jack shrugged. "I really don't know but we have always been different."

Jack sat down at a desk and placed his hands on the table.

"You know," he began, "my brother was always a step behind and to be honest I think it was by choice. When we were in high school he always got in trouble over the dumbest things and I never did. After we graduated I said that we should backpack through Europe, but he didn't want to. He got a job six months out of junior college and married soon after.

"She was nice, but young, you know, like she thought my brother was something he really wasn't…like rich. So, when I left home at nineteen I didn't look back. I sent cards and videos to my brother and mother but never saw a reason to spend much time there.

"Then Tommy came along and boy did I like that kid. I saw him a couple of times a year and sent him e-mails and talked on the phone now and then. He seemed like he had a lot on the ball. It's like he got all of the good parts of my brother and his wife and none of the bad."

"Maybe you should think about seeing your brother," Elizabeth said. "What does he do now?"

"Sits around and complains about life. Just before Mom died she told me he lost his job and then he got fat, smoked and drank too much, and became a nobody. It was like life dealt him bad cards and he didn't play them well."

"That's sad," Elizabeth said.

Jack seemed lost in thought and said, "Sure is."

Shawn returned from the computer lab. "Still nothing?" Jack asked.

"Yeah," Shawn nodded, "we did find a bunch of sites about ancient hoaxes and fake treasure," he shook his head, "stuff we've seen before that has no validity. If we couldn't find it in our data banks maybe it is just a piece of junk?"

Jack smiled and stood up. "All right then," he said, "call Manuel de la Ernesto and tell him we have found his medallion with the blue stone."

"You still want to send the other one to your nephew?" Shawn asked.

Jack thought for a moment, "Yeah, I think he'd like it," the treasure hunter turned to Elizabeth. "Maybe it can bring some good luck to his life."

She smiled and nodded her approval, "Maybe."

CHAPTER EIGHT

Treasure Meeting

Shannon McDougal clicked the mouse for the computer several times before she got to the Internet. She wasted no time working her way to the website she wanted and started to read.

"Next time find me and I will come and get that buffoon off you guys," she said continuing to stare at the computer screen.

The three boys sat at the conference table and looked at one another ashamed. Each one hated the fact that they needed a girl to help them with Zach.

"Shannon," Chris said, "what did you do to Zach? I mean do you have naked pictures of him or something?"

The young girl laughed. "No," she shook her head, "I used to beat him up when we were kids and I think he knows I could still kick his butt so he avoids me."

"I think he likes you," Jackson said. "That could be the only explanation for him never raising a fist to you."

Shannon turned away from the computer screen and glared at Jackson.

"Whether he likes me or not is irrelevant because he knows I could whip him. And you should talk? I don't recall you raising a fist ever."

Jackson looked at Chris and Tommy who nodded.

"She's right," Tommy said.

"Yeah," Chris chimed in, "you never do."

Jackson started to fume, "Can we get this meeting going?"

"Sure," Tommy said. "Shannon, let's go."

McDougal closed down the computer and walked slowly to the round table and flopped into a seat.

"So what are we going to talk about today?" Shannon asked.

"I want to discuss the prospect of going on an expedition," Tommy said.

The group gave him a blank stare.

"Tommy, we've been over this," Chris said. "We don't have any money."

"And we aren't going to get any," Jackson said.

Tommy nodded but replied, "I understand that. All I am saying is let's plan an expedition as if we had money?"

"Then we'd go," Shannon said.

"Good," Tommy replied, "but to where?"

"I think we should go to the Caribbean," Jackson said.

"Why?" Chris asked.

"Think of the amount of gold that was lost because of pirates and smugglers during the late seventeen and eighteen hundreds? And it's sitting at the bottom of the ocean." Jackson shook his head. "It could be worth millions."

"We could rent a charter boat and get all the scuba equipment," Tommy said getting excited, "and then we could go down to the Straits of Florida and Caribbean Sea to check out areas for lost treasures. We could make a fortune and be real treasure hunters like my Uncle Jack."

For a moment no one spoke as they daydreamed about the impossible.

"Too bad it's never going to happen," Jackson said, bringing the dream to an end.

"It could," Tommy said, trying to revive the vision.

"Tommy," Shannon said, "I know that you want us to be real treasure hunters but the truth is we are just kids from a small town who meet to talk about treasure hunting. We've never actually done it."

"I have too," Tommy protested.

Shannon looked at him, "Tommy, going out with a metal detector and finding an ancient soda can is not treasure hunting."

"But it was a TAB," Tommy said. "I don't even think they make those anymore."

"Isn't that the soda in the pink can?" Chris asked.

"Pink?" Jackson said disgusted. "Who would ever use a pink can?"

"My mom used to drink it when she would diet," Chris said.

"But your mom is skinny," Jackson said.

Chris shook his head, "She is now."

"Enough of this!" Shannon screamed. "My God you guys get off track so easily." She turned to Tommy. "Treasure hunting is going to have to wait for us," she said. "I'm sorry."

Tommy looked at the ground. "I know you're right," he said. "I just think the only way out of this place, this house, this town, is through treasure hunting. It's how my uncle got out and he's got a crew, like you guys." Tommy shook his head, "I guess it's pointless. Maybe we should just end this club."

"Wait a minute. We aren't going to do that. We can still talk about things we'd like to find and where they might be," Chris said.

"He's right," Jackson said. "Then we could gather information about them and decide, if we had any money, what we would do to find the treasure. Maybe even talk to your uncle for some help or ideas."

"Yeah, sure. Maybe. Then what would we look for?" Tommy asked.

"How about the Beale Treasure?" Chris said. "Or what about Noah's Ark?"

"Noah's Ark?" Jackson said. "It was made of wood. I am sure it has rotted already."

"You don't think it was made of gold?" Chris said.

Jackson waved his friend off and looked at Tommy. "We could see if those creatures we read about are really alive like the kongamato, the lizard bird, or the olitiau, the bat like creature in Cameroon."

"They're right," Shannon said. "We don't have to end the club because we can't go on treasure hunts. We'll just have to do it in the confines of the club house."

"You guys still want to do that?" Tommy asked.

"Beats going home," Jackson said.

"Besides, this will be good preparation for high school when we have to do research papers and stuff. And you never know, things might change," Shannon said.

"I appreciate all that you guys are doing," Tommy said, "but we are just living in a small town and nothing is going to happen until we leave it."

"Oh, stop that," Shannon said. "I told things can change, it'll just be later that's all."

"No," Tommy said, "I won't stop. I mean my parents are a mess. How can I beat that?"

"Through hard work," Shannon said.

"I could leave and they might never know. Probably wouldn't care," Tommy said.

"Bull. That's a lie," Jackson said.

"Ever see my dad?" Tommy asked.

Jackson nodded, "Okay you've got a point but that doesn't mean you go and leave."

Chris said, "Jackson's right Tommy quit feeling sorry for yourself." He paused unsure how his friend might respond to his criticism. "Your Uncle Jack wouldn't do it."

Tommy slumped in his chair. "I know. I just really want to be a treasure hunter and the possibilities aren't looking very good because I'm here."

"Don't be so sure," Jackson said. "Like Shannon said, 'you never know when something is going to happen that will change your life'."

CHAPTER NINE

Manuel's Medallion

Manuel could barely contain his joy as he held the medallion in his hand like a mother holding a newborn. He turned it over admiring the blue stone.

"You really are the best," he said to Jack.

Jack smiled, "Just doing what I was paid to do, and I had a lot of help."

"You are too modest."

"Manuel, just so you know we found...."

Manuel interrupted, "Jack, I really can't thank you enough for what you have done. The medallion is finally back where it belongs with the Ernesto family."

"Yeah," Jack agreed, "but like I was saying we also found some jewels and old coins that are worth quite a bit. Maybe you would be interested in them?"

"You keep them," Manuel said, his eyes never leaving the medallion.

Elizabeth seemed surprised. "Mr. Ernesto," she began only to be interrupted.

"Please call me Manuel," he said smiling.

"I am so sorry, Manuel, but Jack is right," she said, "we found many good pieces, not just the jewels and the coins."

Manuel waved her off. "I said for you to keep them. A gift from me to you, eh?"

Manuel rubbed the medallion with his thumb and looked at Jack. "This was worth every penny I spent," he said.

"I'm glad," Jack replied. "I must say getting the money was pretty good."

Everyone in the room laughed.

Shawn entered the wheel room and seemed stunned by the number of people.

"I'm sorry," he said. "I didn't know anyone was meeting here."

"No problem," Jack said. "Manuel de la Ernesto, meet one of the finest members of my crew other than Elizabeth, Mr. Shawn Dawkins. He's actually too young to be this good, and unfortunately doesn't have a strong enough memory to remember when I was."

"Pleasure to meet you," the young man extended his hand.

"Likewise," Manuel said and shook Shawn's hand.

"Shawn is the main reason we found such a large cache. He was the leader of the dive and the main operator during the dredge on the bottom of the harbor."

"Then I should send him the check?" Manuel asked smiling.

Jack laughed then turned a mocking serious and said, "You are kidding?"

Manuel laughed out loud again, "Oh, Jack, we need to drink. Get us some champagne." Manuel looked at the medallion studying it more carefully. His eyes narrowed. "These markings are Spanish?"

"What?" Jack asked, "Those? Oh, yeah. To make sure they were a literal translation we ran them through the computer and it reads...here let me see that printout." Jack grabbed a sheet of paper from Elizabeth.

She translated before Jack could read the paper, "It reads 'light into dark' and the other side says 'dark into light.' But I am sure you knew that Manuel."

Manuel smiled weakly and nodded. Elizabeth studied the old man's response and asked, "Do you know what it means?"

Manuel shifted uneasily before he spoke. "Long ago there was a battle over control of light and dark magic. The two groups involved were the Dorcha, followers of the dark magic, and the Leois who followed the light. The Dorcha believed in combining the powers of light and dark but the Leois felt all that power in one place was too much for one person and wanted the two separated. The Leois were able to use a band of gypsies to place the power of light and dark magic into two medallions to safe guard."

"Now you have them both?" Elizabeth asked

"Yes, I do," Manuel smiled.

"But if I recall your medallion doesn't have any writing," Elizabeth said remembering her first meeting with Manuel.

"No, there is not," Manuel said and gave a half smile to the others.

"You mentioned magic," Elizabeth said.

"Yes, magical powers," Manuel said.

"Magic to do what?" Jack asked.

"Whatever is necessary."

Manuel's description of the medallions left the wheel room silent wondering what he meant by his last comment.

Finally Manuel burst out laughing and said, "You don't believe that do you? It is just an old myth. Please, magic in a medallion? How absurd. I got you? No?"

Everyone responded with controlled laughter because no one, other than Manuel, ever heard of such a myth.

"That one does look better than the other medallion," Shawn said.

Manuel's smile faded immediately and his face turned deadly serious, "There is another one?"

Shawn looked confused and said, "Yeah, I thought Jack told you."

"No he did not." Manuel stared at Jack. "Why was I not told this?"

"Actually there were six but four of them were trashed, and the other, well, ah, Jack…" Shawn stuttered nervously and looked to his boss.

Elizabeth sensed something was wrong as she saw Manuel's face change from pleasant to angry.

"Manuel, please understand that we brought up so much stuff, some good, some not so good," Jack began. "I have been studying this kind of thing for years and I know good pieces from bad and that other medallion was worthless. It had these crazy markings or symbols on each side that we couldn't make out and you did say we were the best. I figured that the other medallion was junk so I gave you the better of the two." Jack looked around for help, saw none and continued. "Besides, Manuel, you want the best for your family, and believe me, this medallion is so much better than the other."

Manuel's facial expression never changed, "Did this worthless medallion have a blue stone in it?"

"Yes," Jack said. "As a matter of fact it did."

"And you mentioned crazy markings?" Manuel said his eyes narrowing.

Jack stammered and said, "Yeah, but we couldn't find them in our computer."

Manuel looked at his bodyguards but they did not react. The multi-billionaire glared at Jack who glanced at Elizabeth and Shawn, confused at the sudden turn of events.

"And what did you do with this supposedly worthless medallion?" Manuel demanded.

Jack shrugged, "I sent it to my nephew. Why?"

CHAPTER TEN

A Package Arrives

The UPS driver jumped from his truck. The package he carried wasn't very big and he placed it on the door step, rang the doorbell, and walked back to his van.

Tommy's dad opened the door and cursed at the driver for bothering him, but the driver did not hear him as the brown truck drove off.

Unshaven and wearing the same clothes from the night before, Eric Reed saw the package and picked it up. He glanced at the return address in the corner of the envelope and cringed, his brother.

Eric walked into the house and slammed the door. His wife's eyes opened wide as she sat on the couch trying to blend in, and Eric did not notice her. He headed to Tommy's room.

He burst through the door and kicked the bed where Tommy slept. Tommy jolted up surprised at the unannounced wake-up call.

"What?" Tommy asked startled, his eyes squinting at the intrusive light.

"Here is a thing from your Uncle Jack…again," he said and threw the package on the bed.

Tommy's eyes opened brightly. He didn't want to seem too ecstatic since his dad might get upset, so he nonchalantly grabbed the manila envelope and tossed it on his desk.

"I'll open it later," he said and fell back into bed.

Eric Reed squinted one eye at his son as he picked his teeth with his tongue before screaming at Tommy.

"You know your Uncle Jack is not that special a guy! He left me here and went off running around the world and that's all anyone can ever talk about. When Mom died, your grandma, he didn't bother to show up to the funeral! 'Mr. Globetrotter' is a phony who should be in prison!"

"Dad, he did show up at grandma's funeral," Tommy said. "Remember he spoke at the cemetery."

Tommy's dad stared hard at his son, "Are you saying I am a liar?"

Tommy realized his mistake and said, "No, sir."

"Good," Tommy's dad said. "You just watch yourself. I do not want to see you end up like my selfish brother. Only gives a damn about himself and that precious crew of his. Do you understand me?"

Tommy nodded, afraid to speak.

"Good!" his dad said and walked out slamming the door behind him.

Tommy heard his dad mumbling to himself as he descended the steps, "Should be me out there; not here having to deal with all of this. But he stepped over me and never bothered to ask if I wanted to go…rotten son of a…"

When he heard his dad clear the steps, Tommy leaped from the bed and opened the package like a kid at Christmas. A hand-size medallion with a tarnished blue stone fell onto the floor. Tommy reached inside the envelope and grabbed a handwritten note. "Found something from the bottom of the sea. Uncle Jack."

Tommy couldn't believe it. He stared at the new found treasure and studied every detail of the medallion. These strange markings must mean something, Tommy thought, but they sure are weird looking. And the blue stone needed to be cleaned. He reached for his cell phone and pushed a number.

"Yes, is Chris there?" he asked. Tommy waited a minute until Chris Henderson was on the line. "Chris…Tommy, yeah I'm good. Hey can you meet at the clubhouse…because my Uncle Jack just sent me something and I want the club to see it…great…I will see you in a half hour."

Tommy closed the phone and turned his attention to the medallion. It felt smooth in his hands and he rubbed his index finger over the markings and the blue stone.

Rough, he thought, and he held the medallion closer to his eyes to get a better look at the markings. Sure are different, he thought, like nothing I have ever seen.

He couldn't remember being this excited, except maybe the last time his uncle sent him something. Smiling from ear to ear, Tommy put the medallion on his desk. He felt a new energy to start this day, and got dressed.

CHAPTER ELEVEN

Anger

Jack's wrists burned as the ropes dug into his skin. After learning what Jack did with the second blue-stoned medallion, Manuel had his bodyguards bind Jack and Elizabeth for not giving him information about Jack's nephew.

"Where does this nephew of yours live?" Manuel repeated.

"Do you think I would tell you now?" Jack screamed.

"Then you will pay," Manuel nodded to the largest of his two men and said, "Juan."

The large Spaniard stepped forward and smashed a fist into Jack's cheek. His head jerked to the side and Elizabeth screamed. Jack shook his head and tried to regain his senses after the powerful blow. He spit blood to the floor and said, "Gonna have to do better than that."

"You really think you are some kind of hero?" Manuel asked. "Hit him again."

Juan swung again and connected two shots to Jack's face rocking him back until his head drooped against his chest. Blood dripped from his nose and mouth.

"Manuel, stop this," Elizabeth pleaded her dark eyes puffy from crying.

Manuel looked at the beautiful girl with long black hair and smiled, "Such beauty. You know, Elizabeth, Jack knows that this can end right now if he tells me where he sent the medallion. And of course you could end it also."

"Don't you dare," Jack scolded Elizabeth.

"Your life is on the line, my dear. Let's make a good choice," Manuel said and caressed her cheek.

"I'm sorry, Jack," Elizabeth said as tears formed in her eyes. "It's…it's…" she started to waver, "in the United States!"

Conrado, who'd been watching most of the action, slapped the girl with an open hand snapping her head back.

Manuel smiled, "Funny. But can we suspend the jokes." He walked over to Jack and lifted the treasure hunter's chin. "I want to know where your nephew lives."

"Why? So you can hurt him?" Jack asked.

"Of course not," Manuel said. "But he has the final piece of the puzzle. And since you do not, he is more important. Now why would I want to kill a young boy with such a promising future?"

"I don't get it. What is so special about that other medallion?" Jack asked.

"I told you about the ultimate power that both medallions bring when they are put together. Those crazy symbols, as you have said, are the key to the power that is rightfully mine," Manuel said.   Jack laughed through the pain in his face. "You believe that? Manuel, those kinds of stories are everywhere around this area. You said yourself it is a myth. Come on, Manuel, you never heard of fishing stories? I once caught a fish 'this big,' kind of thing. I would think that a man of your intelligence would not fall for something so stupid."

Manuel slapped Jack across the face and grabbed his blood stained shirt. "Some myths are true, Jack. Just like your blue diamond mine that made you so famous!" He slapped Jack again and walked away.

"Juan, Conrado, let's see if you can't get some answers from these two."

The bodyguards worked over the treasure hunters. After a while Jack could not feel the pain and Elizabeth had been beaten so badly she was barely conscious.

Manuel splashed water on the woman's face and Elizabeth shook her head, trying to focus her eyes without much success.

"I hate to do this to you both, but you are being most uncooperative. Much like your crew," Manuel said.

The comment caught Jack's attention. "What have you done with my crew?"

"They are being taken care of as we speak, my old friend. They didn't seem to know much of anything even when we tried to persuade them. You seemed to keep this very secretive, Jack. Too bad for them," Manuel said and laughed.

"You murderer!" Jack yelled and tugged at the ropes.   "Diamond Jack," Manuel said, "tell me where that nephew is?"

"Not a chance!" Jack spat back.

"Get him again," Manuel ordered and Conrado and Juan slammed their fists into Jack's ribcage. Jack tried his best to absorb the blows but each impact sent waves of pain through his body.

"Have we done enough?" Manuel asked. "Please, Jack, you might as well tell me because if you don't I will find out anyway. You are just making it harder on yourself."

Jack could not form any words, but mustered up the power to shake his head. No.

"Juan, Conrado, tear this ship apart and don't return until you have found the address for his nephew."

The bodyguards went to work on the ship. Cutting apart seat cushions, pulling every drawer out from the main desk and throwing papers all over the compartment. Entering the conservation lab the two thugs took great pleasure in smashing and tipping over all of the water tanks, leaving the floor a mess of water and artifacts.

Elizabeth, now fully awake but hurting, looked at Manuel. "I don't understand why this is so important? The gypsy story is a fake. It's a myth that's all. Why are you doing this?" she pleaded.

Manuel's eyes blazed red and he said, "You will understand in due course."

"Who are you?" Elizabeth stuttered from fear.

"I am Evil as you have never imagined."

CHAPTER TWELVE

A Real Treasure Find

Chris swiped his card and entered the Treasure Hunters clubhouse and found Tommy sitting at the meeting table. Chris's eyes went right to the medallion on the table.

"That's it?" Chris asked a little disappointed.

Tommy seemed confused, "What do you mean 'that's it'? Come on and look at it. My Uncle Jack sent it to me from the bottom of the Caribbean Sea."

Chris picked up the old relic and looked at it quizzically.

"What are these markings?" he asked.

"Not sure," Tommy said. "They are obviously another language but one I have never seen."

"And the blue stone?" Chris placed his finger on it, "What is this?"

Tommy shrugged, "I don't know. A stone. What do I look like, a geologist?"

"No, but shouldn't we know all this stuff before we start calling it a treasure."

"The point is my Uncle Jack, a real treasure hunter mind you, sent it to me for the club and I would appreciate it if you would get a little more excited."

Chris smiled weakly and said, "Yippee."

Shannon and Jackson walked in a minute later.

"Great you guys are here," Chris said. "Look at the new treasure."

Shannon grabbed the medallion first to the obvious disappointment of Jackson. She studied the artifact very closely. "What are these markings?"

"Same thing we were wondering," Tommy said.

"Can I see it?" Jackson asked.

"In a minute," Shannon said emphatically.

"You always say that and…" Jackson stopped as Shannon glared at him and he added, "Why don't you take your time," and sat down.

"I've never seen anything like this before," Shannon said, "and this stone doesn't look like a polished gem."

"Then what is it?" Chris asked.

"Feels like a really rough stone."

"Why put a rock in a medallion?" Tommy asked.

"Don't know," Shannon responded. "Maybe like the markings that we don't recognize, the stone was considered a jewel long ago. Someone did take the time to put it into a medallion. Could be this culture believed that a colored stone held great value or something."

"May I see it now?" Jackson asked politely. Shannon handed it to him and sat down.

"I think I agree with Shannon," Jackson said.

"Big surprise," she said.

"I'm serious," Jackson said. "We don't know what these people took for value. And maybe by putting the stone in a gold medallion it helped a king or something."

"So what's our next move?" Tommy asked.

"I think we go to the library and start our research on the markings and see what we can learn about that stone," Shannon said.

"Why not use the computer here?" Chris asked. "I hate riding my bike that far."

"Our Internet connection is too slow. All of us need to work on this," Shannon said.

"Then let's go," Tommy said and put the medallion in his backpack.

"What are you doing?" Shannon asked.

"What?" Tommy said.

"You're putting the medallion in your backpack?" Jackson asked.

"What's the problem?"

"The problem is you could lose it?" Chris chimed in.

"I will not," Tommy defended.

"Like the original 1913 buffalo coins?" Shannon said.

Leave it to Shannon, Tommy thought, to remember the time, just after the club formed, when Tommy's Uncle Jack sent him a set of the first printed buffalo coins by James Earle Fraser from 1913. Tommy promptly lost the set of coins within an hour of receiving them. However, with the help of Shannon and Jackson they found them in the corn field behind the clubhouse. Tommy still kept a few of the coins in his backpack.

"I guess you're right," Tommy said, "I'll put it in the safe."

"Wait," Jackson said and took out his cell phone and snapped several pictures of the medallion. "There," he said closing his phone and putting it in his pocket, "now we won't have go on memory."

"I could just bring it," Tommy said.

In unison the club yelled, "No!"

After the coin incident the club created a custom-built safe in the bathroom underneath the toilet. The safe had an automatic camera taking still shots of whoever opened the door.

Tommy moved the toilet and worked the combination. He heard the lock click and turned the handle. The door opened and Tommy heard the small snap of the camera as he smiled. He placed the medallion in the safe and closed the door. Spinning the knob on the safe he moved the toilet to its original spot and walked back to the group.

"Is that the first time we've actually used that safe?" Jackson asked.

"For something this big," Shannon said.

"All right then," Tommy said, "let's go."

The Treasure Hunters Club walked out of their clubhouse, got on their bikes, and started the trip to the downtown library.

Inside the safe the medallion started to glow a bright blue. It lit up the entire bathroom in a clear, brilliant color.

*   *   *

Juan rummaged through papers and found a black ledger book. He opened it and found a receipt from UPS.

"Got it," Juan said and he and Conrado walked back to the cabin where Manuel sat waiting as Jack and Elizabeth tried to recover from their beatings.

"*Jefe*," Juan began, "we found this receipt."

"Good," Manuel said and smiled at Jack. "Nice of UPS to put the tracking number on the receipt."

Manuel pulled out his cell phone and began punching numbers. It took only a few seconds for him to connect to the Internet and have the UPS website in front of him. Three minutes later he had Tommy Reed's address.

"I love modern technology," Manuel said as he closed the phone and placed it in his side pocket. "Makes things move much faster don't you think, Jack?"

Jack lifted his beaten face and tried to say something clever but he couldn't. The blood in his mouth wouldn't allow it.

"We need to call our friends and make sure they can have a team in the air within the next hour," Manuel said as Juan began taking notes. "We will need to know when they have made contact and when the medallion is in our possession."

"*Jefe*," Conrado said, "we could take the plane and handle this."

"No," Manuel shook his head. "I need you to take care of other things for me." He turned to Jack and Elizabeth. "I am so sorry it has to end this way, Jack. You are very good at what you do, but alas everyone must someday meet his Maker. And Elizabeth, ahh, another time, another place, we might have been together. But unfortunately it will never be." He kissed her forehead as she turned her head away, every muscle hurting.

Manuel looked at Juan and Conrado, "I want this operation done quickly, make the calls now and let me know when it is done."

"What would you like us to do with them?" Juan asked.

Manuel smiled, "Take them out as far as you can and feed the fishes."

"And the boat?"

"We'll keep that as payment for not completing the job. Okay with you, Jack?"

Jack spit blood on the white tile floor and said, "Sure Manuel, whatever."

"I know," Manuel said and left the cabin.

"What's going to happen now?" Elizabeth asked Jack.

"Well I think we are going to have to become really good swimmers."

They both heard the powerful engines of the boat roar as it started moving out to sea.

CHAPTER THIRTEEN

The Library

The library was located ten miles from Tommy's house and the club weaved and raced through the streets to arrive in only 40 minutes.

During the summer the library underwent a facelift and a new coffee shop was added as well as an expanded audio visual room.

The group swept through the coffee shop and waved to Alice, the manager, as if they were regulars in a bar.

Tommy pointed to the reference sections and the club found a large table to put their backpacks and proceeded to search through the volumes of books.

"I guess we should check under M," Chris said.

"What about L for lost treasure?" Tommy said.

"Very funny, Tommy," Shannon said.

"I'm going to the computers," Jackson said. "This book stuff is going to take too long."

Jackson opened his cell phone and emailed the picture of the medallion to the others.

"Check your email if you need the picture," he said and walked away.

Jackson made his way to the computer section of the library. Thirty computers lined the walls of the spacious room. Jackson signed in at the main desk and sat at the first available computer. He moved the mouse quickly and clicked his way to the Internet.

Tommy, Chris and Shannon poured over books about lost treasure and amazing artifacts.

One book that caught Shannon's eyes was called *Ancient Hoaxes*. She flipped through the pages and read several stories but did not find anything until she got to the last section.

The chapter was entitled "Magical Artifacts" and the first picture staring at her was Tommy's medallion.

She turned the open book to Chris and Tommy and said, "This look familiar?"

Both boys looked up from their books at the same time and stared at the picture. There was the medallion with the crazy symbols and the unique blue stone.

"What does it say about it?" Tommy asked.

Shannon pulled the book back and read aloud.

"'According to legend a gypsy woman was entrusted to protect this particular medallion from the Dorcha, who were followers of dark magic, and she died mysteriously. No one has ever found the medallion or has any idea of its whereabouts.' It also says that 'anyone who has possession of the medallion can tap into its magical powers.'" She looked up at Tommy. "That doesn't sound too bad."

Tommy nodded, "Just keep reading."

"Sorry," she continued, "'After many years of research and study it was found that gypsies used the medallions to frighten people through magic. However, gypsies did not have the ability to use magic in that way'. Your medallion, by the way, was lost during a storm, wait check that, a hurricane in the early 1700s. The markings are an ancient language that no one has deciphered, though it is possibly an extinct Indian tribe, but 'most analysts agree the markings mean nothing.'"

"How can that be?" Tommy said surprised.

"Someone could have engraved them as their own special cipher or something," Shannon said.

"Maybe your uncle just wanted to send you a gift and thought it looked cool," Chris said.

Tommy's eyes dropped. "Man I thought we finally had a real, important artifact."

"Oh, Tommy," Shannon said. "This is just a starting point. We have more research to do."

"Or," Tommy shrugged, "we might as well take it to the exhibits at the Civic Center."

"You love that exhibit," Chris said amazed.

"I do, but I really thought this might be our first treasure for the club."

"Actually you could probably sell the medallion to Mr. Thornberry, the director of the exhibit. He's always looking for new stuff," Chris said.

Shannon shook her head and said, "Wait until we learn more about the medallion, Tommy. Someone thought it was important 300 years ago."

His friend's comments did little to help Tommy's mood. The rush he felt when he received the medallion dissolved and he closed the book he was reading and got up from the table. "I'm going to get a drink," he said.

"All right," Chris said his eyes returning to a book.

"Tommy," Shannon said, "are you going to be okay?"

Tommy nodded and walked away.

"Nice sensitivity," Shannon said to Chris.

"What? That?" Chris said surprised, "He'll be fine. I say we head to the Mythological Artifacts Exhibit and sell it."

"Always money with you," Shannon said shaking her head.

"What good is it to be a treasure hunter if you are always poor?"

"Whatever," Shannon said dismissively.

Jackson came down the hallway carrying four sheets of paper.

"I found it," he said and handed the papers to Shannon.

"Yeah," she said as she leafed through the black and white pictures exactly like the ones in the book, "we've already read about it."

"No way," Jackson said surprised.

Both Shannon and Chris nodded.

"Then you know about the gypsies?"

"Yes."

"And the dark magic?"

"Yes."

"And the special magic put into the medallion that we have?"

"Yes."

"And the *second* medallion?"

Neither answered.

"What second medallion?" Shannon asked.

"You mean I found out something the great Shannon McDougal did not?"

"Just tell us," Shannon said firmly.

"Let me enjoy this for a second," Jackson said as a satisfied grin swept across his face.

Shannon lost her patience and rose from her seat, "You've got two seconds before I beat it out of you."

Jackson realized his moment was over and said, "According to what I found the gypsies were asked by a group called the Leois to put the power of magic into two medallions."

"We only read about one," Shannon said.

"What kind of magic?" Chris asked.

"The power of light or dark."

"Power of light or dark?" Shannon said.

"Yeah," Jackson picked up the papers and started to read, "The Leois were afraid the Dorcha…"

"Followers of the dark magic," Shannon interrupted.

"Yeah," Jackson said, "the Leois believed that combining both sides of magic would create some kind of super power that no one group should be in control of. So they had the gypsies separate them."

"And?" Chris said as he stood looking very interested.

"You know one medallion has a blue stone and the other a red," Jackson said.

"Red?" Chris said.

"It has the dark magic inside it," Jackson said, "you know evil."

"So if it's separated what is the big deal?" Shannon asked.

"If you do this," Jackson clasped his hands together and said, "and put the two medallions together," he paused.

Shannon and Chris remained silent and stared at Jackson. "Yeah?" they both said.

"Followers of the Leois and Dorcha believed you would have the ultimate power for good and evil," Jackson said.

"So we don't have the other medallion and that makes ours worthless?" Shannon asked.

"Not necessarily," Jackson said. "From what I read on the Internet a single medallion was thought to have some magical properties just not as much power as if you had the two, but I didn't find out what kind or how to use it."

"In the book *Ancient Hoaxes* it talked about the person in possession of the medallion being able to use its magic," Shannon said.

Tommy walked back to the table carrying a can of pop.

"Hey, Jackson," he said, "find anything?"

"I'll say," Shannon said and handed the papers to Tommy.

"What are these?" Tommy asked as he put the can of pop down.

"Just read them and look at the picture," Shannon said.

Tommy started to read and couldn't believe his eyes. He stopped and stared at the group. He felt a wave of energy flow through him. "This is unbelievable," he said and continued reading.

"Do you believe it's true about the magic?" Jackson asked.

Tommy shrugged. "Let's keep working to find out."

*　　　　　*　　　　　*

The Gulf Stream jet landed and taxied to an empty hangar in a deserted part of the small airport.

Two men emerged from the plane; both built strongly, one with brown hair named Gavin and the other with darker hair named Dillon.

A black Mercedes pulled up and a driver got out and handed Dillon the keys.

"Here's the address," the driver said handing a slip of paper to Dillon.

"Photo?" Gavin asked.

"One in the car."

"All right," Dillon said and motioned for Gavin to get in. They quickly sped toward the exit and onto the highway.

CHAPTER FOURTEEN

Fish Food

Water splashed the side of *Hanoj* as the boat sped out to sea. Juan piloted while Conrado guarded the prisoners.

Jack started to wiggle his hands free and started to feel the rope loosen even as it dug deeper into his wrists with every turn. Though it burned Jack refused to accept the circumstances of the situation. When he got Elizabeth's attention he motioned for her to try to free her hands but she returned a defeated look which only fueled Jack's resolve.

"Conrado, bring up the first drop off," Juan said.

Conrado smirked at Jack and walked down a companionway to a big refrigeration facility on the boat. He grabbed a large object sealed in a plastic bag, flipped it over his shoulder and walked back to the main deck.

Jack saw Conrado carrying the bag and asked, "What's that? Dinner for you two?"

"No," Conrado said, "just a friend of yours." Conrado flipped the plastic bag over his shoulder and it landed with a thud on the deck. Conrado unzipped the plastic and Jack looked inside.

It was Shawn Dawkins.

"Look familiar?" Conrado asked.

The motors stopped and the boat started to pitch with the gentle waves.

Jack's anger boiled as he looked at Shawn.

"Mr. Ernesto thought you would want to die with your friend," Juan smiled broadly, "and of course the girl as well."

Juan picked the lifeless Shawn Dawkins up and threw his body off the deck. The loud splash made Elizabeth wince.

Conrado pulled out two sets of ankle weights and showed them to Jack and Elizabeth.

"Who's first?" Conrado asked.

"The great treasure hunter," Juan said to his partner. "I'll cover you." And he removed a .38 caliber pistol from his coat.

Conrado bent down and wrapped the weights around Jack's ankles. Jack judged them to be about fifteen to twenty pounds. Conrado then turned his attention to Elizabeth who sat quietly resigned to her coming doom.

"Elizabeth?" Jack said.

She looked at him with sorrowful eyes.

"Don't give up yet," he said.

"Why?" she asked.

"Because," Jack yelled and his right arm swung free and slapped the gun out of Juan's knuckles.

Jack freed his other hand, grabbed the chair and smashed it across Juan's chest, causing pieces of splintered wood to fly everywhere.

Jack felt a foot connect to his back and he fell to the ground. He bounced up quickly and smashed a right cross to Conrado's jaw dropping the large man. Jack swung around and caught Juan in the midsection with a powerful kick. Both bodyguards rolled on the ground in pain.

Jack ran to Elizabeth and untied her hands just as Conrado and Juan regained their footing. In one moment each person noticed the gun lying on the floor and dived for it. Bodies smashed against one another as the gun slid across the deck.

Juan grabbed Jack and swung a fist at his face. Jack slipped out of the way and Juan's hand connected with Conrado's nose. Blood shot out and Conrado's eyes closed quickly as he slumped to the ground.

"My nose!" he yelled as his hands covered his blood-soaked face.

Still holding Jack by the shirt Juan slammed him several times against the wall. Jack's body started to go limp in Juan's large paws.

The click of a cocking gun caused Juan to stop.

Elizabeth held the .38 revolver and seemed quite comfortable with it. She did not shake as she pointed it at Juan and gave him a steely-eyed stare.

"Let him go," she said.

"You wouldn't dare," Juan said smirking.

Elizabeth moved the gun slightly and fired. The bullet whizzed past Juan's head and hit the console.

"Try me," she said.

Conrado attempted to stand but could not. His injury caused his eyes to swell shut and blood poured out of his nose.

"Drop him Juan and pick up Conrado. He needs your help," Elizabeth said.

Juan reluctantly let go of Jack who shook his head, straightened his shirt and nodded at the large Spaniard.

"What's next?" Jack asked Elizabeth.

"Time to see if these boys can swim," she said.

"You are not going to throw us in the water?" Juan asked.

"Of course not," Elizabeth said.

"Good," Juan said as he steadied Conrado.

"Both of you are going to jump in," Elizabeth said and smiled.

Jack grabbed the used rope and wrapped it around Juan and Conrado. He pulled them closer to the edge of the boat.

"Any last words?" Jack asked.

"We are not going to jump," Juan said defiantly.

"No problem," Jack said and pushed the two bodyguards off the side. He turned to Elizabeth with a wink and said, "Let's go."

Jack pulled the cord on the compressed gas cartridge of a yellow raft and tossed it over the side where it inflated.

"Rowing 35 miles will keep them busy," he said.

Jack stood at the console and turned the key. The engines roared and drowned out the screams of the two in the water as Jack pushed the gas and headed back to Port Royal Harbor.

"We need to get a hold of Tommy before Manuel does," Jack said.

"Can we call from here?"

"No. You shot the radio, Liz," Jack said. "And the beasts destroyed our cell phones."

"We'll call when we reach port," Elizabeth said. She paused, "Do you think he already got to Tommy?"

"I hope not," Jack said and revved the motor for more speed.

CHAPTER FIFTEEN

Surprise Guests

Tommy watched his friends ride away as he stood in his driveway dreading the next moments. He knew his father probably spent all day stewing about his life while Tommy's mother worked quietly around the house trying not to upset anyone or thing.

Tommy thought for a moment about continuing to ride but he didn't. He parked his bike, took a deep breath and walked in the front door.

"Where have you been?" his father snapped.

"The library," Tommy said, placing his backpack on a wooden bench.

"What for?"

"Just looking up stuff."

"With those friends of yours?

Tommy's dad never liked anyone and especially resented Tommy's friends. Not that he ever got to know them or their names, Tommy thought. However, Tommy's dad constantly complained that each of them was a spoiled, misbehaved brat. Once Tommy tried to argue, got a swift slap, and never spoke about it again.

"Yeah, Dad," Tommy said. "What's for dinner?" trying to change the subject.

"Your mother made something," Eric Reed said as he rose from his chair and slowly walked into the kitchen.

"Hey Mom, what are we eating?"

"Rigatoni with garlic bread," she said.

"Great," Tommy said, trying to sound excited.

Dinner at the Reed house used to be fun. Tommy's parents once got along, told funny stories, but as Tommy grew older, times changed. His father lost his job and seemed to drift while his mother retreated inside herself. A cold silence laced its way through every meal.

Tommy sat at the side of the square table with his mom at one end near the stove and his dad at the other. The rigatoni looked great and Tommy dug in. Pasta was one of his favorites and he was starving, so almost anything would have tasted good.

Tommy's dad ate a few rigatonis, slammed a beer and got up without finishing his meal. He grumbled under his breath, walked into the family room and turned on the television.

"I saw you got a package from your Uncle Jack," Tommy's mom whispered.

"Yeah," Tommy said, careful not to raise his voice too loud.

"What was it?"

"Just some fake artifact Uncle Jack says he found at the bottom of the Caribbean Sea."

"Must be nice there," his mom said as her eyes gazed out the window.

"Not as fun as here," Tommy said with a smile, trying to cheer up his mom.

She looked at him and smiled the way mothers smile at their sons, "I guess not," she said. "Are you finished?"

"Yeah, thanks."

Tommy's mom grabbed his plate, placed it on hers and walked to the sink to wash them.

Both turned their heads to the sound of the doorbell.

Eric Reed answered the door in his usual rude way.

"What do you want?" he yelled.

Two men in suits and wearing sunglasses smiled. One flashed his badge so quickly Tommy's dad didn't really think he saw anything.

"Hello, is this the Reed residence?" the brown haired man asked.

"Who wants to know?"

"I am agent Gavin with the FBI and this is agent Dillon."

"Yeah, so?"

"Are you the father of one Thomas Reed?" Dillon asked.

"Is he in trouble?"

Both men laughed. "No, not at all. We just have some questions to ask him," Gavin said.

Tommy's dad shook his head, "Boy has got trouble with the government now. Tommy, come here, these men want to talk with you."

The phone rang. No one from the Reed family attempted to get it even after three rings.

"Pick it up, will ya!" Tommy's dad yelled to his wife.

Tommy walked through the family room and saw the two men dressed in black. They wore sunglasses, which Tommy thought strange since the sun was almost down.

Tommy heard his mom pick up the phone and say "Hello…yes, he's here."

Just before Tommy reached his dad in the doorway, his mother yelled for him to get the phone. Tommy looked at the two men and decided he should take the call first. He picked up the cordless phone in the family room.

"Hello," Tommy said and heard a click as his mother hung up.

"Tommy?" the voice seemed hurried.

"Yes."

"It's Uncle Jack."

Tommy's eyes lit up, "Hey, I was just…."

His uncle quickly cut him off, "No time for talk, Tommy. Did you get the medallion I sent you?"

"Yes."

"Have you told anyone about it?"

"Just the club."

"Tommy, you must listen carefully at what I'm about to say. Don't freak out or anything. I need you to be treasure-hunter-cool, okay?"

"Okay."

"You are in great danger because of that medallion," Jack said.

Tommy heard the words "great danger" and froze, his eyes fixed on the men talking to his dad at the front door.

"So what do I do?" Tommy whispered.

"Hide the medallion," Jack said. "Guard it with your life. If anyone comes looking for it, make up some story, but do not let it go."

"All right," Tommy said. "I think some people are here now."

Jack breathed deeply into the phone, "Say nothing. I am on my way. Be safe."

Tommy held the phone to his ear and waited for a dial tone.

"Let's go, boy, these men are busy," his dad yelled.

Tommy put the phone in its holder and slowly walked to the front door.

"Hi," Tommy said and even managed to smile.

"Thomas Reed, I am agent Gavin and this is agent Dillon and we are with the FBI," he said flashing his badge quicker than the eye could see.

"You can call me Tommy. Am I in trouble or something?"

"No, Tommy you're not," Agent Gavin said. "We just need you to answer a few questions for us."

"Okay."

"About your Uncle Jack," Gavin emphasized.

"Now *he* should be arrested," Tommy's dad blurted out.

Tommy stared at his dad in anger and then remembered what his uncle said about treasure-hunter-cool, "Sure I can answer."

"When was the last time you saw your uncle?"

"About a year ago."

"When was the last time you spoke with him?" Dillon asked joining the conversation.

"I haven't," Tommy said. "I got an e-mail from him a week ago. It said he was in the Caribbean doing an excavation."

"Has he sent you any packages recently?" Gavin asked.

Without missing a beat Tommy said, "Yes, would you like to see?"

Gavin gave Dillon a nod of confidence.

"Definitely," Gavin said.

"It's in my book bag," Tommy said and started rifling through the notebooks and folders. He unzipped a pocket where he kept some of the buffalo coins Jack sent him long ago.

"Here," Tommy said holding the four coins in the palm of his hand. "Pretty cool, huh? These are actually originals printed in 1913."

"Was that what that UPS guy dropped off the other day?" Tommy's dad said turning to the agents, "Woke me up from my nap."

"Right," Tommy said relieved, "The UPS package. That's it."

Gavin and Dillon's surprised expression was not lost on Tommy who plowed ahead.

"If these are stolen you can have them back. I don't want to get Uncle Jack or myself in any trouble."

Both men looked at the coins stunned.

"No," Gavin said, "that isn't what we are looking for."

"Then what?" Tommy asked. "I mean if I know what it is maybe I could help."

"A medallion," Dillon said.

Tommy's insides jumped at the word but outwardly he remained calm. "Sorry, sirs, but Uncle Jack has never sent me anything like that."

Gavin nodded and said, "Well then, thank you for your time. We are going to check out some other leads around town."

"Okay," Tommy said as he felt sweat forming on his palms.

"We'll check back in a couple of days," Gavin said, "in case the medallion should arrive."

"If it does I'll hold it for you," Tommy said and smiled.

"Goodbye," Gavin said as Dillon waved and followed him to the car.

The door shut and Tommy breathed a sigh of relief. His dad walked to the couch, grabbed the remote and resumed watching television.

Tommy peered through the drapes as the two men got in their car and drove away. Stepping back from the window Tommy noticed his shaking hands and prayed he didn't do such a thing in front of the two men.

"I told you my brother was no good," Tommy's dad said.

Tommy looked at his dad and then returned to the window. His hands wouldn't stop shaking and he wished they would.

CHAPTER SIXTEEN

Fleeing

Tommy couldn't get to the clubhouse fast enough. He punched the numbers to Chris's house into the phone and waited.

"Hello," Chris said.

"Chris, it's Tommy."

"Hey, long time no see."

"Can you come over?"

"It's getting late," Chris said, "we just finished dinner."

"I know but something has happened and it's about the medallion."

"What about it?"

"I can't tell you over the phone. Just come over and call Shannon and Jackson too."

"You're starting to sound weird," Chris said. "Are you in some kind of danger?"

"Just get everybody and come over," Tommy said and closed the phone.

Tommy walked toward the small safe and stopped. What if the medallion were really magical? Could he handle such a thing? But why would Uncle Jack send something that would get him in trouble? Tommy wondered. Besides, what would he do with a magical medallion anyway?

Many questions, Tommy thought, and no answers. Tommy stepped into the bathroom and moved the toilet. He pressed several numbers on the keypad and waited to hear the lock click open. Tommy grabbed the medallion and looked quizzically at it. The blue stone in the middle looked so small. Could something that size actually possess magic? And those markings? Was it a magical saying from long ago? Tommy ran through more questions before deciding the medallion didn't seem all that magical. In fact it seemed rather ordinary.

He turned it over in his hands. He stared closely at the markings. Uncle Jack must know what they mean, Tommy thought. But why wouldn't he tell me over the phone? I know he wouldn't put me in danger.

The knock on the door startled Tommy and he dropped the medallion. Picking the medallion off the floor Tommy looked at the video security monitors and saw the FBI agents with his dad standing outside.

Tommy stuffed the medallion into his pocket, closed the safe and put the toilet back into its place.

Another knock and Tommy's mind started to race. He had to get out of the clubhouse.

Tommy moved the sink and stared at the man sized hole that led to the underground tunnel the group created. He was against building it because he could never imagine any kind of emergency that would require him to slip out this way. Now he softly thanked the others for insisting on an escape route, just in case.

Tommy slipped easily into the tunnel and pulled the sink back into place behind him and started the long crawl. The group originally wanted tunnels large enough to stand up in but without any money they were happy to have a crawl space.

The tunnel stretched one hundred yards to the middle of a cornfield behind Tommy's house. It belonged to the farmer two miles down the road.

Tommy lifted the plank covering the tunnel and he stepped into the twilight and was surrounded by corn. He put the board over the hole and looked in the distance. He could see by the fading sunlight the outlines of his father and the two agents. As he stared down the road leading to his house he could just make out three familiar bike riders. Tommy sprinted through the tall corn hoping to cut off Chris and the others before they reached the clubhouse.

*　　　*　　　*

"I heard him come out here," Tommy's dad said and slammed his fist on the door. "He's always out here."

"That's all right," Gavin said holding his temper.

"You guys came back awfully fast," Mr. Reed said.

"We had some questions we forgot to ask Tommy. But now that we know he spends a lot of time here, we'll know where to find him. Thanks."

Gavin and Dillon walked back to their car. Gavin pulled out his cell phone and punched a button. In an instant Manuel was on the phone.

"Yes sir, we've made contact," Gavin said and paused. "No, we don't have the medallion yet but we are confident that we will have it in the next couple of days." Gavin paused again. "We know, no collateral damage, yes sir…okay; goodbye." Gavin closed his phone and put it in his jacket pocket.

"What did he say?" Dillon asked.

"He said take care of this quickly."

*   *   *

Tommy came through the cornfield and looked down the road. He saw the silhouettes of his three friends riding their bikes toward his house. He ran at them as fast as he could.

"Is that Tommy?" Shannon asked.

"Why is he running?" Jackson wondered.

Tommy waved his arms frantically. "Hide," he yelled, "hide."

When Tommy reached the bikers it took him a minute to catch his breath.

"What is it with you?" Chris asked.

"My…." Tommy took a deep breath and continued, "My Uncle Jack called and," Tommy breathed deeply again, "he said that the medallion has put me in danger. Then these two guys show up at the house from the FBI and…."

"Wait," Shannon interrupted, "the FBI?"

Tommy glanced over his shoulder and saw the black Mercedes pull out of his driveway.

"In here," he screamed and pushed Shannon and her bike into the cornfield as Chris and Jackson followed.

"Get down," Tommy said lying on top of Shannon.

"From what?" Shannon said. "And get off me!" She pushed him to his side.

"Just shh," Tommy said.

It seemed like hours but the car sped past the group a minute after the Treasure Hunters Club hid in the cornfield. Tommy got up as did the others and they brushed the dirt and corn leaves off their clothes. Each walked to the street and stared hard at Tommy.

Tommy didn't notice their looks and said, "My Uncle Jack called and told me to hide the medallion. I don't think those are FBI guys, but they kept asking if Uncle Jack had ever sent me any packages."

"What did you tell them?" Jackson asked.

"Why do you have to hide the medallion?" Shannon wondered aloud.

"One thing at a time," Tommy said. "I told the two guys he had sent me stuff and I showed them the old buffalo coins."

"The buffalo coins?" Chris said surprised.

"Yeah," Tommy said and looked over his shoulder to see if anyone was coming.

"Then what?" Jackson said.

"So they left and I went to the clubhouse and called Chris."

"Then why rush to meet all of us out here?" Shannon asked.

"Because after I talked to Chris those FBI guys came back and went to the clubhouse pounding on the door."

"How'd you get out?" Jackson asked.

"The escape tunnel," Tommy said.

Jackson smiled. The tunnel had been his idea. "You mean you actually used it?"

"Do you have the medallion?" Shannon asked.

"Yes," Tommy said.

"So what are you going to do?" Jackson asked.

"Chris, can I stay at your house tonight? Tell your parents we have a big project due tomorrow at school."

"I'm sure it will be okay," Chris said.

"But what about tomorrow?" Jackson asked.

"My Uncle Jack said he was on his way. So I will go to school as usual."

"Why?" Shannon wondered.

"It'll be the safest place until my uncle arrives."

*   *   *

That night Tommy pulled the covers over his shoulders and tried to close his eyes. His mom said it was all right for him to stay at Chris's house and didn't bother to tell Tommy's dad. She knew it would be easier for her son.

"Tommy?" Chris asked from across the room.

"What?"

"Is it really magical? The medallion I mean?"

Tommy pulled the medallion from under his pillow and examined it once again.

"Doesn't seem so."

"I figured," Chris said, disappointed.

"Me too," Tommy agreed.

All this trouble and the medallion doesn't even have any magic, Tommy thought, nice piece of treasure, Uncle Jack.

CHAPTER SEVENTEEN

The Safest Place

Tommy walked off the bus at Kennedy Middle School and scanned the parking lot looking for the black Mercedes but found nothing. Tommy could feel the FBI guys out there. Chris walked in front of Tommy without a care in the world.

A hand touched Tommy's shoulder and he jumped, dropping his backpack. It was Jackson.

"Are you all right?" his friend asked.

"Yeah, just a little nervous," Tommy said smiling and he shouldered his pack.

"How did it go last night? Did you sleep?"

"Not much," Tommy said.

A bell rang signaling the students to get to their first-period class.

"I'll see you at lunch," Jackson said.

"Let's get to Mr. Sims' class," Chris said. He turned to go and stopped when he saw the look on Tommy's face.

"It will be safe in here," Chris said. "Your Uncle Jack will be here soon and no one is going to get you in school."

"What about Zach?" Tommy said.

Chris thought for a moment and said, "Good point but at least we know Shannon can take Zach. Let's go."

Tommy reluctantly agreed and the two friends walked into the middle school, hoping to have an ordinary day.

Tommy fell into the school day as he normally did. Moving between classes had become so routine by this late in the school year that he could probably get to class with his eyes closed, he mused.

However, Tommy still couldn't help being nervous. Like in art class when he fell out of his chair when the phone rang. This drew much laughter from everyone, including himself.

Still, Tommy walked the hallways keeping an eye out for Agents Gavin and Dillon. At one point he thought he saw them and dove into the bathroom only to discover the two men were janitors.

It was during this bathroom hideaway that Tommy ran into an even bigger problem, his old friend Zach Butler.

"Hey there, Tommy boy," Zach said.

Tommy turned around as his eyes fixed on the big eighth-grader standing before him.

"Oh, hi, Zach," Tommy said. I think he grew since yesterday, Tommy thought.

Zach lumbered toward Tommy, "I think we have some unfinished business."

"Too bad I can't stay," Tommy said and dove to the ground, did a summersault and fell into the hallway before getting on two feet and sprinting away. Tommy heard Zach mention something about lunchtime but he was gone so fast he wasn't sure.

*　　　　*　　　　*

Jackson and Chris met up with Tommy just outside the cafeteria doors with a bully update.

"Coast is clear," Jackson said.

"Zach got in a fight last period. He'll be in school suspension the rest of the day," Chris said.

For the first time Tommy felt some relief. He put his hands in his pockets and felt the medallion. All this for a piece of junk that doesn't have any magic, Tommy thought, shaking his head in disgust.

After getting their lunch the group sat at a table near the exit. Tommy positioned himself with his back to the other students so he could see who walked in and out of the lunch room.

Tommy choked down several bites of the school's pizza when he felt a massive hand on his shoulder. He wanted to turn but the strength of the hand held him still.

"Thought I'd forgot about you," the familiar voice said.

Jackson and Chris stared at their food. Tommy slowly turned his head and said meekly, "Hi, Zach."

"I think I'll take that pizza," Zach said and grabbed the slice off Tommy's tray. "You probably don't need this milk either." Zach chugged the carton down and dumped a plate of green beans into Tommy's lap.

"Oops," Zach said laughing. "I'm sorry."

Tommy pushed himself away from the table. "You know what?" he said his temper rising.

"What?" Zach said stepping closer to Tommy.

Tommy looked at the hulking beast before him and said, "Nothing."

"Mr. Butler," a teacher interrupted, "you are not supposed to be here. Now say goodbye to your friends and get back to the suspension room."

"Goodbye," Zach said, "friends."

"So long," Jackson said cheerfully.

Zach walked away looking at other people to torment before leaving the cafeteria.

"I'm sick of this," Tommy said, "I wish we could…."

"What?" Chris asked.

"I don't know," Tommy thought for a moment, "dump a large vat of strawberry jelly all over him."

As the words left his mouth Tommy felt a sharp pain in his leg. The stone from the medallion started to burn into his flesh.

Tommy sat up straight unsure of what to do. He reached into his pocket then stopped as the intensity of the burning increased. Tommy winced in pain as the stone grew hotter.

Jackson noticed first. "Tommy, what's wrong?" he asked.

"I don't know," Tommy said as he clenched his teeth in pain. "But the medallion is setting me on fire," and he slumped to one side.

"Then take it out," Chris yelled.

With the pain rising Tommy reached into his pocket and pulled the medallion out. It burned his fingertips but he could not let go of the medallion.

Tommy's eyes squinted as the blue stone glowed brightly casting off rays of florescent light.

All three boys sat transfixed by the unique blue beams scanning around the room, but no one else noticed.

The loud scream from the hallway got everyone's attention. Zach staggered back into the lunchroom covered in strawberry jelly. The students erupted with laughter and cheers.

Tommy looked at the medallion. The glowing blue stone faded as well as the heat. He quickly put it into his pocket. Tommy scanned the lunchroom and noticed that everyone had resumed to their earlier conversations.

"What just happened?" Chris asked.

"I don't know," Tommy said.

"Maybe that thing is magical after all," Jackson said.

Tommy watched as Zach was led out of the room with a long trail of jelly following him.

"Well if it is," Tommy said, "I like that kind of magic."

Everyone at the table smiled and agreed whole heartedly.

*   *   *

The second to last period of the day was English. For Tommy it was one of the most boring classes. Not that the teacher wasn't any good, Tommy just didn't like the subject.

Five minutes into the "find a verb" lesson the classroom phone rang. Tommy didn't move. The familiarity of school and the enjoyment of watching Zach Butler covered in strawberry jelly calmed him a bit though he remained tense.

Mrs. Palmer spoke into the phone, "Yes he is…okay," she said and hung up. "Tommy they need you in the office."

All eyes looked at Tommy as his stomach did summersaults.

"Thanks, Mrs. Palmer," he said and walked out of the classroom.

*　　　　　*　　　　　*

Mrs. Palmer's room was on the other side of Kennedy Middle School so the long walk gave Tommy time to think about what awaited him in the office.

No one liked going to the office, Tommy thought. Nothing good ever happens when you are summoned. More often than not things go from bad to worse or more worse.

Tommy reached the end of the hallway and looked at the windowed office. The principal's door was closed. Then it finally hit Tommy, his Uncle Jack was here. He felt relief and his steps picked up as he went down the hall.

Ms. Weathers, the secretary, directed Tommy to a chair while Principal Diggs finished with his business.

Tommy felt a smile creep across his face. He couldn't wait to see Uncle Jack. He would know how to handle the entire situation. Tommy thought that maybe Uncle Jack would take him on a treasure hunt. The thought brought a tingle to the back of Tommy's neck. For the first time he wasn't thinking about his pursuers or his father just the fun and joy that came from seeing his Uncle Jack.

The door to the principal's office swung open and the balding, overweight Mr. Diggs emerged.

Tommy smiled at him but Mr. Diggs did not return it.

"Mr. Reed, please come in and have a seat."

Tommy stood and walked past the principal into the spacious office.

Two steps inside, Tommy stopped. He didn't see his Uncle Jack sitting there. He saw the FBI agents, Gavin and Dillon.

"Hi there, Tommy," Gavin said. "Got a minute?"

CHAPTER EIGHTEEN

A Magical Moment

Tommy's heart leaped in his chest. The two so-called FBI agents sat before him in the one place Tommy never dreamed they would be: the principal's office. Maybe they are FBI agents, Tommy thought. How else could they get in here?

"Tommy, please sit down," Mr. Diggs said and Tommy sat in a cushioned chair as Mr. Diggs went behind his large oak desk. The principal left the door open.

"Now," Mr. Diggs cleared his throat before beginning his lecture, "it is my understanding that you have some information that these men, FBI agents by the way, need. Tommy, you have never been in trouble and I know that you want to do the right thing. It is your duty as an American and a student of this school to uphold the character traits that we consider important in building a society…."

Mr. Diggs continued but Tommy already tuned him out. His eyes darted around the room looking for an escape, some place he could get away from these guys. The looks on Gavin's and Dillon's faces gave Tommy pause; they must know I have the medallion, he thought. I could wish for more strawberry jelly, but how many times can that happen? Tommy thought. His mind pondered various ideas all of which made him more scared.

As Mr. Diggs droned on Tommy began to consider giving the men the medallion. It's really not magical, he thought, no matter what happened in the lunchroom or with the glowing stone. Tommy looked out the window. Where was his Uncle Jack, anyway?

"So, finally," Mr. Diggs was ending his long speech, "Tommy, could you please cooperate and give these gentleman what they need?"

Tommy looked at Mr. Diggs and then at Gavin and Dillon as if he were seeing them for the first time.

"I'm sorry, what?"

"That's it," Dillon said and stood. Gavin put his arm out and Dillon sat back down.

"Tommy, all we need is what your uncle sent you," Gavin said, "then we'll leave you alone and you can go about your life."

"I showed you what he sent me," Tommy said. "It was those buffalo coins. That's it."

Tommy slipped both hands into his pockets as his left gripped the medallion.

"Tommy," Dillon spoke with controlled fury, "we need the artifact. Your uncle stole it from an important excavation and made you an accomplice to his crime. We talked to your dad…."

"Which would lead you nowhere," Tommy said smartly.

"He knows your uncle a little better than you do, kid," Dillon said. "Now quit playing games!"

Tommy grew angry as he thought of all of the lies his father probably told. He's jealous, Tommy thought, because he never did anything with his life.

"If you aren't going to cooperate then we have no choice but to place you under arrest," Gavin said.

"Arrest?" Tommy said and gripped the medallion tighter. If he could only disappear and find his Uncle Jack all of this would be better. He needed to be invisible.

In the palm of his hand Tommy felt the blue stone begin to warm. Tommy started wishing harder that he were invisible.

Tommy noticed the aghast looks on the three men's faces as they seemed to stare straight through him. Tommy looked around to see if he had missed something.

"Where did he go?" Dillon asked.

"Tommy if this is some kind of trick you are only making it worse on yourself," Mr. Diggs said rising from his seat. "It is time to stop this nonsense."

It took Tommy several seconds to realize the medallion had worked again. He'd vanished into thin air.

Mr. Diggs screamed for Ms. Weathers.

"Yes, sir," she said entering from the outer office. Tommy saw his chance and bolted for the open door.

"Has Tommy Reed run or maybe crawled past your desk in the last ten seconds?"

"No he hasn't."

I just did, Tommy thought, and he made his way to the outside office door.

"If you see him report to me immediately."

"Of course," Ms. Weathers said and turned to go back to her desk when she screeched, "There he is!"

Tommy looked at her and his blue eyes widened. Principal Diggs, Gavin and Dillon ran to the doorway.

"Get him!" Gavin yelled.

Tommy opened the outer office door and sprinted down the hallway.

Gavin and Dillon nearly trampled Ms. Weathers as they toppled over her trying to get to Tommy. They jumped up quickly and sprang after the young Mr. Reed.

CHAPTER NINETEEN

Diamond Arrival

Jack and Elizabeth wasted little time getting from their plane to the Rent-a-Car desk. In ten quick minutes they drove through the airport exit and headed for the highway.

"That lady at the desk was helpful," Elizabeth said.

"Yes, she was," Jack said as he pushed down on the pedal and speeded up.

"She said Kennedy was only fifteen minutes from here. Old place look familiar?" Elizabeth asked.

Jack shrugged. He really could not remember much about his hometown. Everything seemed new and yet oddly familiar to him even though he hadn't been back to his home state in over a year or was it two, he wondered.

"I just hope we can find Tommy," Jack said waiting at a red light.

"You told him we were coming," Elizabeth said. "I am sure everything is fine. He's in school. What could happen?"

Tommy ran as if his feet had wings. He took the steps down to the cafeteria and ducked inside the boiler room home of the janitorial staff and their student helpers.

Tommy saw Marcus Evans, a student assistant, holding a dripping mop over a bucket of water.

"Marcus," Tommy said out of breath.

"You in a hurry?" Marcus asked.

"Sorta," Tommy said looking around for a place to hide. "There are some people following me and I can't let them find me."

"Mr. Diggs one of them?"

"Yes."

"Hate that guy," Marcus said. "Hide by that last furnace there. It'll be hot but no one ever goes back that far and they won't be able to see you."

"Thanks," Tommy said and worked his way over pipes, old paint cans and rusted volleyball poles to the far furnace. He crouched down and wrapped his arms around his knees. The noise in the room would be good cover, Tommy thought. Still, he measured his breaths so they weren't too loud.

He stopped breathing when he heard the boiler room door burst open.

"Who is this?" Gavin asked.

"He's a student assistant," Mr. Diggs said. "Marcus, we are looking for Tommy Reed. Have you seen him?"

"No," Marcus said, "I was just getting a mop to clean up the cafeteria."

"If you see him please report it to the office. It's very important," Mr. Diggs said as he and Gavin ran through the cafeteria and back up the stairs.

*   *   *

Jack parked the car in the front parking lot of Kennedy Middle School and he and Elizabeth walked quickly to the front door.

"Did you go to school here?" Elizabeth asked as they entered the main office.

"Yeah," he said. "But when I went here it was a high school not a middle school."

Ms. Weathers emerged from the office mail room and said, "May I help you?" and sat behind her desk.

"We are here to see Tommy Reed," Jack said. "I'm his uncle."

Ms. Weathers shook her head. "He sure is popular today."

"What do you mean?" Jack asked.

"Well, two FBI agents and Mr. Diggs just had him in the office and apparently," Ms. Weathers looked around to see if anyone was listening before whispering, "he snuck out and 'disappeared,'" Mr. Diggs said.

"Disappeared?" Elizabeth said and looked at Jack.

"The medallion," Jack said softly. "Do you know where he is now?"

"They are looking for him in the building," Ms. Weathers said.

"Let's go," Jack said and pushed Elizabeth to the door leading to the main hallway.

"Hold it," Ms. Weathers screamed. "You are not allowed to run these hallways without permission from Principal Diggs so if you would kindly take a seat before I call security, I will get him."

Jack and Elizabeth stopped moving and politely sat down.

"Never thought this would happen," Elizabeth said.

"What? The FBI guys being here?"

"No," she said. "That I'd be back in the principal's office."

*   *   *

Tommy poked his head up and saw the door shut. Marcus continued ringing out the mop. Tommy worked his way back toward Marcus.

"Thanks," Tommy said.

"No problem," Marcus said. "I would never tell Mr. Diggs anything. The guy is an idiot."

"Yeah," Tommy said his mind racing with ideas. "Do you think you can get a message to Chris Henderson? He's in Mrs. Palmer's English class right now. Room 10."

Marcus shrugged. "Sure, what's the message?"

"Hang on," Tommy said and unzipped his backpack.

He fished out a spiral notebook and opened to a blank page. He started writing symbols in neat rows.

Marcus saw the writing and asked, "That's a message?"

"Yeah," Tommy said as he finished the last symbol. "It's called monoalphabetic substitution cipher. It was used by the Freemasons during the Revolutionary war to encrypt their messages and keep them from the British."

"Oh," Marcus said very unimpressed.

"Here get this to Chris Henderson," Tommy said and ripped the piece of paper out of the notebook and handed it to Marcus.

"Consider it done," Marcus said. "Room ten?"

"Room ten," Tommy said and watched Marcus leave.

Tommy headed back to his hiding place praying the message would get to Chris.

*　　　*　　　*

The walkie-talkie on Mr. Digg's belt crackled as Ms. Weathers' voice came through. "Mr. Diggs, please pick up."

Diggs smiled half-heartedly at Gavin and Dillon and pulled the walkie-talkie from his belt.

"Yes."

"I have a Jack Reed here to see Tommy. Have you found him yet?"

Gavin paused as the name Jack Reed registered in his mind.

"No, but we will continue looking." Diggs looked at Gavin and Dillon. "I could force the school into a lockdown mode and get the police here."

Gavin and Dillon's eyes went wide, "No need for that," Gavin said. "As a matter of fact, we should be calling into headquarters with an update. Just want to thank you, and we really have taken up enough of your time."

"It's no trouble," Mr. Diggs said when he noticed Marcus walking by. "Hey, Marcus, anything?"

"No," the young man said and continued down the hallway to room ten.

"Who was that?" Dillon asked.

"Already talked with him," Gavin said dismissively. "Mr. Diggs, thanks for your help." He grabbed Dillon by the arm and said, "Let's go."

The two men walked down the stairs and out a side door near the bus port.

"Gentlemen, you can go out the front door," Mr. Diggs said as the glass door slammed shut.

Mr. Diggs held the walkie-talkie close and said, "Tell Mr. Reed I'll be right there."

*   *   *

Marcus handed the note to Mrs. Palmer who handed it to Chris. Chris opened the folded piece of notebook paper and saw the symbols. He flashed it toward Shannon who simply nodded.

*   *   *

Gavin and Dillon ran to the car.

"Why did we get out of there so fast?" Dillon asked.

"Didn't you hear?" Gavin said. "The kid's Uncle Jack is in there."

"So Diamond Jack Reed is here." Dillon said looking at the school.

"Get in. We need to call Mr. Ernesto and tell him the situation."

"Why?" Dillon asked as he got in the passenger seat.

"Because Reed is supposed to be dead and since he's not, I think we have bigger problems."

The black Benz pulled out of Kennedy Middle School and drove away.

Mr. Diggs came down the hallway and entered the main office.

"This is Jack Reed, Tommy's uncle," Ms. Weathers said, "and this is his aunt?"

"No," Elizabeth said. "I'm Elizabeth Haden, Jack's assistant."

Ms. Weathers rolled her eyes, "Of course you are."

"Please come into my office and we can talk," Mr. Diggs said.

Jack and Elizabeth walked in the office and this time Mr. Diggs shut the door.

Chris and Shannon huddled together in the hall after class ended.

"Let me see," she said grabbing the note.

"He used the cipher," Chris said. "You got the key?"

"Yeah," she said as she looked at the symbols.

"Where are you next?" he asked.

"Math. You?" Shannon fished out a small spiral notebook from her backpack.

"Social Studies," he said.

"Where is Jackson?" Shannon asked as she folded the paper.

"AP Chemistry," Chris said. "Since I've got Social Studies, give me the message and the key."

"Here," Shannon handed the note and the notebook to Chris. "When you find out what it says let me know."

"Okay," Chris said and hurried to Mr. Crist's Social Studies class.

*   *   *

After checking the identification of Jack and Elizabeth, Mr. Diggs smiled, "How can I help you?" he sat down behind his enormous desk.

"I understand some men came to see Tommy today," Jack said.

"Yes and I must tell you I was very disappointed in how Tommy reacted."

"Why?"

"I can't get into it but the men were FBI agents and they were asking him questions and he wouldn't cooperate. Very unlike him."

"Questions about what?" Jack asked.

"You," Diggs said. "Something that you sent him in the mail was a stolen artifact from some excavation."

"Stolen?" Jack said surprised.

"Yes. And the two gentlemen wanted it back."

"These FBI guys," Jack said, "did they give their names or a card on where to reach them?"

Mr. Diggs smiled, "I must tell you that I am reluctant to give you much information, Mr. Reed."

"Why is that?" Jack asked annoyed.

"If you have done what they say, then you are a criminal and I do not want to be an accomplice in any way."

The comment caused Jack to stand.

"Just tell me where Tommy is?" Jack insisted.

"I think we need to keep our temper," Mr. Diggs said, surprised by Jack's sudden emotion.

"Are you going to tell me?"

Diggs waited a moment and said, "We are still looking for him."

Jack turned to Elizabeth and said, "Let's go."

They started for the door but Elizabeth stopped and walked back to Mr. Diggs desk.

"You never said the names of the FBI agents or if they gave you a card," she said while flashing her dazzling smile.

Mr. Diggs smiled back, "Gavin and Dorey or Darryl something like that."

"And a card?"

Diggs shook his head, no.

"FBI agents with no cards," Elizabeth said. "That should have been a red flag," and she walked out the door with Jack.

Mr. Diggs felt slighted and yelled, "They did have badges!" But Jack and Elizabeth were already gone.

*   *   *

Chris looked at the message and saw Tommy used the pigpen cipher, which used symbols to replace letters.

Chris waited to decode the message until Mr. Crist started a movie. Opening the note from Tommy, Chris studied the symbols carefully.

Chris flipped through the notebook in the near darkness until he came to the page with the key grid used to decipher this type of message. Tommy must have been in serious trouble, Chris thought, for him to use the cipher. Using the key, it took Chris several minutes to translate the code. He looked over the letters stunned.

THEY R HERE.

BACK OF SCHOOL.

END OF DAY.

Chris closed the notebook, folded the paper and put it into his pocket. Chris got up and asked Mr. Crist if he could use the restroom.

Mr. Crist, retiring at the end of the year, didn't care if any students stayed in class or not, so he granted the request.

Chris walked to Shannon's math class and knocked on the door which Mrs. Cribbs opened slightly.

"The office needs Shannon McDougal."

"Shannon," Mrs. Cribbs said. "Office."

Chris and Shannon walked a few steps down the hallway and stood beside some lockers out of view from passersby.

"Well?" Shannon asked excitedly. Chris handed her the note. He looked around nervously as if the men could jump out at any moment.

Shannon read the note and said, "They are here? Those FBI guys?" She started to look around.

"Relax," Chris said. "When class is over we'll meet in the main hallway."

"Why?"

"Because Jackson will be finishing his AP class and we can all go out the gym doors. It's a short cut to the back of the school."

"I guess," Shannon said unimpressed.

"Scared?" Chris asked.

She straightened up and said, "Nope. You?"

"Ah," Chris said and walked away, not wanting Shannon to know about the knot in his stomach.

Shannon turned to go back to Math feeling the same way.

The bell rang to end the day and Shannon and Chris grabbed their stuff from their lockers and hustled to the main hallway. They met Jackson and pulled him aside.

"Read this," Chris said, handing him Tommy's note.

Jackson's brown eyes blinked quickly behind his glasses. "Where are they?"

"We don't know," Chris said, "but let's get behind the school as quick as we can."

"Hey, where is your buddy?" Zach Butler yelled from the other side of the hall.

"None of your business, Zach," Shannon said.

Zach approached her and for the first time he did not seem intimidated.

"You don't scare me, Shannon," the brute said.

"Zach, if I wanted I could mop this floor with you and not even break a sweat."

Chris and Jackson stepped away as the two combatants were now face to face.

"I'd like to see you try," Zach said.

Shannon's eyes narrowed and she clinched her fists. This would be fun, she thought, and then she remembered Tommy.

"I've got to go but this isn't over," she said and turned to leave.

"I knew you weren't that tough," Zach said and a broad smile slipped across his face.

"Yes I am," Shannon said and did a quick reversal and approached the smiling bully. She pulled back her right fist and slugged him in the gut.

Chris and Jackson looked at Shannon with surprise and pride. Zach dropped like a sack of dirt.

Shannon stood over the fallen beast. "Don't ever bother me or my friends again."

Zach barely muttered a word as he gripped his stomach and prayed for relief.

Shannon looked at Chris and Jackson and winked. "Come on." The two followed as she led the way.

The three club members walked down the hall to the gym and made a quick left exiting through a side door. They saw the bus port busy with students getting on their busses. Shannon, Chris and Jackson scanned the crowd hoping to find Tommy and praying they didn't see his pursuers.

"You see him?" Jackson asked.

"No," Chris said. "But there are a lot of people out here."

Shannon looked across the street, "I don't see the black car. Maybe they left."

"Guys," Tommy said emerging from behind some bushes drenched with sweat, his clothes sticking to his body, as if he had played in the rain.

"What happened to you?" Jackson asked.

"I'll explain later," Tommy said. "We can't use my house so we'll need to use the back-up."

"My house," Shannon said somewhat surprised. "Why?"

"Those FBI guys are sure to have someone at my house, but not yours." Tommy said.

"Never thought this would happen," Chris said.

"Then let's move," Shannon said.

The group blended into the crowds of kids, got on Shannon's bus and started for her home.

Chris tapped Tommy, who was slumped down beside him, "Where is your Uncle Jack?"

"I don't know," Tommy said. "But we sure could use his help right now."

CHAPTER TWENTY

Anger and Reluctance

Manuel answered his cell phone after the second ring. It was Gavin. As Manuel listened he grew angry. How could two of his top people fail to handle a teenage boy?

"So what do you plan to do?" Manuel asked.

"Well," Gavin stammered sensing the disappointment in Manuel's tone. Gavin's next statement caused him to tremble for fear of Manuel's reaction. "There is something else."

"Of course there is," Manuel said disgusted. "What is it?"

"Diamond Jack Reed is here."

There was silence on the line. Manuel could not believe it. That could only mean that his bodyguards, whom he trusted to take care of Jack and his assistant, were dead.

"I see," Manuel said softly.

Neither man spoke for a few moments until Gavin started mumbling something about revenge but Manuel cut him off.

"It seems I must take care of this personally. I will be on my plane later today. Please be at the airport to pick me up."

Manuel closed his phone and threw it across the room. "Damn you Jack Reed!" he screamed.

Gavin closed his phone, looked at Dillon and said, "He'll be here tonight."

*   *   *

Jack waited at the stoplight impatiently. With his worst fears realized Jack felt unsure of his next move. He cursed himself for not finding out more in the beginning about Manuel and now he'd put Tommy, someone he cared for, in danger.

"Do you have any ideas?" Jack asked. The light turned green.

"Yes I do," Elizabeth said with confidence.

"What?" Jack seemed eager to hear.

Elizabeth gave Jack an all knowing look. It took Jack several seconds before he realized what this particular look meant.

"No," Jack said.

"Yes," Elizabeth insisted.

"No, no, no," Jack shook his head emphasizing his disapproval.

"Why not?"

"Because it will be pointless. It always turns into a big fight and I don't think we have the time to waste with him."

Elizabeth breathed deeply, collected her thoughts and said, "Jack, he is your brother whether you like it or not. And his son is in trouble. It is your duty to tell him!"

"My brother doesn't care."

"He might. Besides, we need help finding Tommy. Maybe he has some ideas on where to look. We sure don't have any."

The car came to a stop sign. Jack did not accelerate the car. He just sat mulling over Elizabeth's comments.

"Well?" Elizabeth asked.

"Left to the house and right to…I'm not sure," Jack smiled.

He waited for traffic to clear and turned left.

"I know this might be tough, but maybe it can bring the two of you closer together," Elizabeth said.

"There is too much history between us," Jack said. "And old grudges die hard in my family."

"We are still going to need his help to find Tommy."

"My brother can barely help himself let alone his son."

"We need him," Elizabeth insisted.

"Why is that? I mean I understand telling him his son is in trouble but do you really believe he knows anything?"

"He knows Tommy's friends," Elizabeth said. "I figure Tommy is with one of them."

"How do you know?"

"He's a teenager," she said. "He won't trust adults, so his friends are the only ones."

"I guess," Jack shrugged.

"How about him disappearing?" Elizabeth said.

"Yeah, that medallion must really be magical. No wonder Manuel wanted it so bad. That means the myth is real."

"Do you think he knows by now what happened to Juan and Conrado?"

"I would say yes and he is none too happy about it. I'm guessing that's why those two guys are after Tommy. I was so stupid to leave the UPS receipt in the open."

"It wasn't your fault Jack. I never trusted Manuel from the start."

They drove in silence for several more miles. Finally, Elizabeth patted Jack on the knee.

"We'll find him," she said hoping to reassure Jack and more importantly herself.

*   *   *

The Gulf Stream jet took off just after four. Manuel's pilots informed him they should arrive around seven, weather permitting.

Manuel sat by himself and stared out the window. With Jack back in the picture things became more complicated, he knew. Manuel wondered if Jack realized the awesome power the medallion possessed. More importantly, would he know how to use it? And what of this teenage punk who was able to elude one of his best hit teams? He needed someone new, someone who could handle this situation without Manuel's guidance. Someone who could disappear without a trace after the job was done.

Manuel pulled his cell phone from his pocket and punched some numbers. He waited until he heard a male voice say, "Hello."

"Yes," Manuel said. "I did not think you would be needed but I was wrong…tonight after seven…no problem." Manuel closed his phone and for a brief moment felt relief.

Jack pulled the car into the driveway and stopped.

"I can't do this," he said.

"Sure you can," Elizabeth reassured.

"He and I will end up fighting and it's always about the past and all that. I'm not doing it."

Elizabeth heard enough, "Then don't!" she yelled. "Jack, I have listened to stories about your brother and I have been sympathetic but this isn't about you two. Tommy is in trouble and he needs our help. So suck it up, swallow your pride, and let's go and ask your brother for help finding his son. If you can't man up, then I'll do it myself!"

Jack was flabbergasted. She never spoke to him like this, and yet, he knew she was right. Manuel and his goons would continue to dog Tommy until they got what they wanted and Jack knew they wouldn't hesitate to kill anyone standing in their way.

He turned the key and the car shut off.

"Good," she said. "Come on," and got out of the car and headed for the front door.

Walking up two steps to the porch Elizabeth looked over her shoulder. Jack wavered in the driveway. Elizabeth motioned for him.

Reluctantly Jack walked up to the porch.

He tried to smile and said, "It's about Tommy."

Elizabeth nodded and knocked on the door.

CHAPTER TWENTY-ONE

Research Surprises

Shannon McDougal's house stood in a cul-de-sac with four houses on each side. Her parents admired her toughness and strength of character. They also did not mind the time she spent with the other treasure hunters, though she was the only female member.

What Shannon's parents did not know was that their house was the official "back-up" clubhouse for the Treasure Hunters Club.

The finished basement of the McDougal house had a traditional bar and entertainment center. Off in a separate room was Mr. McDougal's office which had an elaborate computer system that could rival a software company. This became a real advantage to the group if they needed information in a hurry. However, they didn't like to use the "second" clubhouse for fear of Shannon's parents overhearing their meetings.

When the group arrived at Shannon's home they scurried past Mrs. McDougal with a quick hello and ran to the basement taking seats on an old couch.

Tommy settled in and told the rest of the group the story of his day. They sat mesmerized by the tale.

"You *disappeared?*" Shannon asked.

"That's impossible," Jackson said.

"I'm telling you it happened," Tommy stressed. "What about the strawberry jelly thing with Zach."

"What?" Shannon asked.

"You didn't hear?" Chris said. "Tell her."

A broad smile came across Tommy's face. "Well, Zach's all over me in the lunchroom and I'm getting mad but I'm not going to do anything so I wished he had strawberry jelly dumped all over him."

"And it happened?" Shannon said in disbelief.

"Just crushed him with it," Tommy said. "But right before it happened, when I was wishing, I felt the stone in the medallion start to heat up and burn."

"That's one crazy story," Shannon said.

"All right then, what do we do now?" Chris wondered.

All eyes fell to Tommy.

"We need more information about this medallion," Tommy said pulling it from his pocket. "I'm still not sure why my Uncle Jack would send this to me if he knew it might lead to trouble."

"Maybe that's why he sent it," Chris said.

"Chris is right," Shannon said. "He probably thought it would be safer with you."

"Then why did he call?" Tommy questioned.

"He must have figured out, too late unfortunately, that there was trouble associated with the medallion," Shannon said.

"Out of curiosity, where *is* your uncle?" Jackson asked.

*　　　*　　　*

Unshaven, clothes dirty and holding a beer can, Eric Reed opened the door and stood before his brother and Elizabeth. He shook his head in amazement.

"Boy you must be in real trouble if you came here," Eric said laughing. "Milly come and see what the wind blew in."

Milly came out from the kitchen and forced a smile.

"Hello, Jack," she said. "What a pleasant surprise. Please come in."

"Yeah," Eric said, "by all means come in."

Jack and Elizabeth walked in and stood in silence. Eric shut the door, walked past them and into the family room. He took a slug of beer and plopped down onto his recliner.

"I'm sorry," Jack said embarrassed. "Milly, this is Elizabeth."

"Nice to meet you," Milly said.

"Like wise."

"Can I get you two anything, coffee, tea, a pop?"

"We're fine," Jack said.

"Well sit down," Eric yelled from the next room. "And tell us about the trouble that brought you back here."

"I'm not in any trouble, Eric," Jack snapped.

"You're the rich one so you can't possibly need money and from the look on your face you know we don't have any."

"I don't have a look," Jack said getting impatient. He entered the family room. "But now that you mention it, how about getting off your lazy ass and…"

"You calling me lazy in my own house?" Eric stood up from his chair, his fists clenched.

"Right now I am," Jack said and he faced his brother.

Elizabeth stepped between them. "All right that's enough of this from both of you. Now sit down."

The brothers stared at one another for several moments before sitting.

"Thank you," Elizabeth said. "Now I am sure that you two have plenty to talk about but that is for another time. We need to know where Tommy is."

"You got him mixed up in your life?" Eric said shaking his head. "That's why he's wanted by those two FBI guys."

"They are not FBI agents," Jack said.

"Well they had badges," Eric said.

"Sure they weren't plastic toys?" Jack said sarcastically.

"You know you are not that big that I still couldn't whip your butt," Eric said.

"Eric," Elizabeth stepped in again, "do you know where Tommy is?"

"Spent the night at a friend's house. Not sure who."

"Chris Henderson," Milly said softly.

"Do you know where he lives? Or an address?" Elizabeth asked.

Embarrassed Milly just shook her head.

"Eric," Jack said, "your son's life is on the line here, please give me something to help him."

After a long pause Eric said, "If Tommy was in trouble, he would come to me. He's always in that old camper out back. He's got it locked up pretty good, but if you can get in there you might find something."

"Thanks," Jack said.

"Milly, show them where it is," Eric said and cracked open another beer. "My boy knows how to take care of himself. I did teach him something you know."

Elizabeth and Jack followed Milly through the kitchen and out the back door.

"Is Tommy gonna be all right?" Milly asked her eyes starting to well with tears.

"Yes, Milly," Jack said. "I won't let anything happen to him."

"Jack, about Eric," Milly shook her head.

Jack raised his hand, "It's not your fault, Milly. That stuff goes back a long way between the two of us."

Milly put her hand on Jack's and squeezed before walking back into the house.

Jack turned to Elizabeth and said, "Let's go in and find something useful."

*   *   *

Tommy and Shannon worked on her father's computer while Chris and Jackson studied the medallion.

"Nothing," Shannon said frustrated.

"Keep at it," Tommy encouraged.

"I keep getting sites about strange magic but the articles make no sense and are written by amateurs. And you can forget about any information that has to do with those symbols. They don't exist."

"What about hurricanes and bad storms, stuff like that?" Tommy asked.

"According to a site about the history of Port Royal Harbor, sixteen major hurricanes were reported between 1712 and 1951. So we know there were bad storms but it wasn't like the people in Jamaica kept accurate records. There could have been more than sixteen. And there is no mention of any medallions," Shannon said shrugging her shoulders.

Tommy stared at his computer screen not sure what to do next.

On the other side of the basement Jackson wrote out the symbols on large sheets of paper and studied each one.

"Is that helping?" Chris asked.

"Just give me a minute," Jackson said.

Jackson couldn't comprehend the symbols. They did not seem to come from any time period he knew about. The problem had him stumped and frustrated.

Finally he blurted out, "They just don't make sense!"

"Maybe they aren't supposed to," Chris said.

"What?"

"I mean maybe they were just carved there so the medallions would have symbols."

"No," Jackson said shaking his head. "How do you explain the strange things that happen with it? Those symbols mean something magical and we need to find out what."

"Ahh," Shannon yelled from the computer room, "nothing!"

Silence pervaded the room. The adventure the group wished for was nothing like what they'd imagined. People were trying to get them, maybe even kill them and the sense of helplessness they felt caused them all to feel deep frustration.

Tommy couldn't help but remember things his uncle told him about treasure hunting and felt a surge of energy to fight on.

"Guys," Tommy said, "my uncle always said 'when the puzzle proves too great that's when, a real treasure hunter will emerge.' We've got to dig in and keep going. The answer is out there just waiting to be found but it isn't going to be easy."

Tommy's words and look of determination gave the rest of the club a renewed sense of purpose and they pressed on.

"Try this," he said and typed a word into the computer search engine for Shannon to see.

Chris saw his friend's new excitement and followed suit, "Let's start over," he said to Jackson.

The group started working again and reaffirmed what they knew about one another. No matter the problem they would always keep trying.

*　　　　　*　　　　　*

Jack examined the key pad lock and smiled. Couldn't have done better myself, he thought.

Jack used a thin metal rod to poke inside the lock. He turned it several times until he heard a click and saw the green light flash on the key pad.

"And I thought we'd have to break it down," Elizabeth said as she walked through the door.

Once inside the veteran treasure hunters stood amazed at the setup.

"This is nicer than ours," Elizabeth said.

"Look at this," Jack said staring at a wall adorned with maps. "Tommy marked everywhere I've been."

"What's all this?" Elizabeth asked pointing to a shelf with small artifacts on it.

"Some of the stuff I sent him over the years," Jack said as he grabbed an old Spanish coin and smiled. "Remember this?"

"Sure," Elizabeth said. "It was my first dredge."

"Seems so long ago," Jack said.

"It was, Jack," Elizabeth said strongly.

They looked around the camper for several more minutes and found nothing.

"Kid's got some great books," Elizabeth said admiring the small library.

"Any address books?" Jack asked.

"I don't see any."

Jack glanced at a photo on the wall. He grabbed it and stared. These must be the people Tommy talks about, Jack thought. In the picture three young people stood next to Tommy who held a pink soda can. TAB, Jack smiled and wondered if they still made that drink? He turned the picture over and read the inscription. "Our first treasure find. Treasure Hunters Club, Tommy, Chris, Jackson and Shannon. "

"It's them," Jack said and showed the picture to Elizabeth.

"Just the first names," Elizabeth said as she took the frame.

Jack grabbed a book off the shelf. "Here is their yearbook. See if you can match the pictures with the names."

"Sounds like fun," Elizabeth said.

"Then get the names of their parents and use that computer to find them," Jack said.

Elizabeth flipped through the pages quickly, her eyes scanning the pictures.

"Done," she said with a satisfied smile.

"You sure do work fast," Jack said impressed.

"I know," she said and sat down at the computer and clicked her way to a search engine. She started typing.

"What are you doing?" Jack asked.

"The system has a security wall so I'm circumventing it."

It took Elizabeth five minutes to find all of the Treasure Hunters Club parents. An Internet white pages site gave her the phone numbers and addresses. Elizabeth turned off the computer and motioned for Jack to follow her out the door.

"Let's go and find your nephew," she said confidently.

CHAPTER TWENTY-TWO

Angry Arrival

Gavin and Dillon waited in a large hangar at the far end of the small airport. All private charters came this way since most millionaires and billionaires did not have time to be subjected to airline security measures.

The Gulf Stream V taxied its way to a stop. After a few moments the door dropped open and out stepped Manuel de la Ernesto. He did not look happy.

"Senor Ernesto so good to see you again," Gavin said.

Manuel eyed Gavin and Dillon with disgust. "If you two had done your job I wouldn't have to be here."

"Our car will take you to the motel," Gavin said as he opened the back door and Dillon gathered the luggage from the plane. "It's pretty primitive out here."

Once Manuel was in the car they headed for the exit.

"I am sure I don't have to tell you how disappointed I am with you both," Manuel said. "I have lost two of my best men and you tell me that the medallion, which was within my grasp, is still held by some kid!" Manuel clenched his teeth. "I should have you both killed."

"We were sorry to hear about Juan and Conrado, Mr. Ernesto, but we have a plan that will get the medallion back in our hands."

"And what is that?"

"It seems Tommy Reed hangs out with a group of friends, three to be exact, and we figure by putting the heat on them, he'll easily give up the medallion."

"And what about Diamond Jack?"

"Well," Gavin said and looked at Dillon who shrugged.

"Mr. Ernesto," Dillon said, "we thought, well, maybe he would realize his nephew is in danger and back off."

That made Manuel laugh.

"You obviously do not know Jack Reed," he said.

"Yes, sir," Gavin said, "I think we do and…"

"I have heard enough of this," Manuel said cutting off Gavin. "Gentleman, it is time to call in a professional, a man who can get things done and not leave a trace. Someone with a way of blending into the background after a job is finished. A real professional."

"Who is that?" Dillon asked.

"Slider," Manuel said.

Gavin and Dillon looked at each another.

"Do we need to take such a drastic step?" Gavin asked.

"He's right, sir," Dillon said. "We can handle this."

"I do not believe it. Besides, Slider and Jack Reed have such a lovely history. It would be so nice to bring the two of them together again."

"They know each other?" Gavin asked.

"For years. Slider wanted to be greater than the famous Diamond Jack Reed and for a while it looked like it might happen. Slider found himself about one hundred yards away from one of the greatest silver bar caches in the west but Jack beat him to the loot. Jack's legend grew larger while Slider slipped into obscurity, before, of course, he took up his new profession of quietly fixing people's problems."

"That's one way to put it," Dillon said.

"He considers himself a problem solver," Manuel corrected, "and we need this kind of problem solved."

"I still don't think we need Slider," Dillon said.

Manuel waited a few moments before he spoke.

"Gentlemen, Slider will be much more motivated than the two of you. Your services will certainly be needed but as decoys. Slider will handle the more dangerous acts. You don't understand the importance of this medallion. It is time to turn up the pressure on this kid." Manuel smirked and added, "And his uncle, too."

The men did not talk the rest of the way to the motel.

Gavin pulled the car to the front of the motel as Dillon stepped out to help Manuel.

Manuel got out of the car and grunted, nothing like the luxury the rich man was accustomed, "Get my bags," he said and walked into the lobby.

Dillon waited for Gavin to open the trunk before getting the bags.

As the two walked into the motel Dillon leaned over to Gavin and said, "If he's calling in Slider, how are we supposed to help?"

"I don't know," Gavin said. "Let's just hope Slider let's us."

"Is he really that good?" Dillon asked.

"I've never met him, but the stories I have heard about him are quite impressive."

CHAPTER TWENTY-THREE

Decisions

"Well that's the best I can do," Shannon said as she threw an encyclopedia on the pile of references books that surrounded her.

"I can't believe we aren't able to find any more information than the basics," Tommy said. "Anything with you, Chris?"

"I'm tapped," Chris said. "But Jackson isn't finished trying."

Jackson Miller's genius was being put to the test. He loved moments like these, but the frustration of not being able to solve this puzzle angered him.

"Why not just go to the police?" Shannon said.

"With what?" Tommy asked before he mocked himself with a conversation of one. "Yes, officer, I have a magical medallion that two men are trying to kill me for."

"Don't think they'd believe you?" Shannon asked with a smile.

"I think when someone hears 'magical' in a sentence they turn you off," Tommy said.

"We could go to your parents," Chris said.

Tommy looked at his good friend. "I'm sorry, Chris, have you met my parents?"

Chris thought for a moment and said, "I guess you're right. I'm sorry for bringing it up."

"What about Uncle Jack? Isn't he supposed to be on his way?" Shannon asked.

"He was, but I don't know where he is and since my cell is broken I have no way of getting in touch with him."

"You can use mine," Shannon said.

"Why can't you use a land line?" Chris asked.

"We could, but my Uncle Jack's cell number is in my phone and it doesn't work," Tommy said.

"You can't remember it?" Shannon said smiling.

Annoyed Tommy said, "No, I can't."

"Hey guys," Jackson said from across the room. He stared at the computer screen and waved his hand to the others, "I think you need to see this."

*　　　　　　*　　　　　　*

The car carrying Jack and Elizabeth turned right and slowly merged with traffic.

"It's not the Miller kid," Elizabeth said. "Try Henderson next and then McDougal."

Jack nodded and said, "The good news is we only have two more to go. The bad news is if he isn't at either place, we have no where else to turn."

*　　　　　　*　　　　　　*

"What is it?" Tommy asked as Shannon and Chris followed him to Jackson's work area.

"It's a website for mythological artifacts," Jackson said.

"Yeah, so?" Chris said.

"So?" Jackson said annoyed. "Look," he pointed at the computer screen. The blue-stoned medallion filled the monitor.

"Is that?" Shannon asked.

"Sorta," Jackson said.

"What do you mean sorta?"

"This place only deals with replicas of mythological artifacts."

"What does it say about the medallion?" Shannon asked.

"Nothing," Jackson replied. "The website is under construction but maybe we can find an e-mail or something?"

"Wait a second," Chris said, eyes widening. "The Exhibit of Mythological Artifacts. Tommy, we saw this medallion there. Remember? There was an entire display of medallions."

Tommy thought for a moment and said, "We saw Thor's hammer, the iron sword that can fight without a man, Achilles' shield and those arrows used by the Roman god for something, but I really don't remember any medallion display."

"That's where we can get the information," Jackson said. "We can see if they have a duplicate of your medallion."

Chris jumped in and said, "I told you they have one."

"Even if the museum doesn't have a duplicate, maybe someone at the exhibit will know what the markings mean," Shannon said.

"I think it's time we take a trip to the exhibit," Jackson said.

*   *   *

"What is the house number?" Jack asked Elizabeth.

"Fifty-five fifty-one," she said.

"There it is," Jack pointed and parked the car next to the curb.

Both got out and headed for the front door.

"Let's handle this better than the Henderson's," Elizabeth said.

"Hey, I thought he was lying and I didn't like his attitude."

"You threatened him."

"Yeah, well," Jack stammered, "he was not very nice."

"Be that as it may," Elizabeth said, "I will do the talking to the McDougals."

Elizabeth approached and rang the door bell.

"This has got to be it," Jack said.

"It better be," Elizabeth said. "This is the last house."

*   *   *

In the McDougal basement all of the treasure hunters shouted out ideas about what to do with the medallion until Shannon finally had enough.

"That's it!" she yelled. "How long will it take us to get to the Civic Center?"

"I'd say thirty minutes," Tommy said, "but that's if we take the main roads."

"Okay, then thirty minutes," Shannon said.

"Wait a second," Chris said. "If we take the main roads those guys are sure to see us."

"He's right," Jackson said.

"How much more time would it take us if we took the back roads?" Shannon asked.

"Another fifteen or twenty minutes," Tommy said.

"So an hour?" Shannon reasoned.

"Looks like it," Tommy replied.

Shannon started up the stairs to tell her mom she would be leaving when she heard voices at the door. She stopped and heard a man's voice ask for Tommy. She ran back down the steps.

"There are people at the door," she said.

"It's those FBI guys," Tommy said.

Shannon looked at Tommy. "What do we do?"

"The walk-out door," Tommy pointed to a door that led to the McDougal backyard.

"Bikes are on the side of the house," Chris said.

"We can cut through the Torrence yard and avoid the main streets," Jackson said.

Quietly the group walked out the door and went for their bikes.

Mrs. McDougal shifted on her feet nervously before asking, "What is it you want with Tommy? And how is my daughter involved?"

"I am sorry, Mrs. McDougal, but my nephew is one of her friends and I need to know where he is."

"Tommy Reed is your nephew?"

"Yes," Jack said.

"You're the Uncle Jack or what was it? Diamond Jack?"

Jack smiled, "Yes, that's right."

"Why didn't you say so," she laughed. "I have heard so much about you from Shannon. You are quite the super hero."

"Thank you but if we could just see Tommy," Jack said.

"No problem. Come on. I'll show you where they are."

Elizabeth and Jack followed Mrs. McDougal to the basement.

As they descended the stairs she said, "They don't spend too much time here but when they do, they come down to the basement and," she stopped.

No one was there.

"They were just here," she said.

"Where did they go?" Elizabeth asked.

"They must have gone out the side door," Shannon's mom said.

"To where?" Jack asked.

"Don't know," Mrs. McDougal said. "When they get on those bikes they could end up anywhere."

"Bikes?" Elizabeth said looking at Jack. "Then they can't get far."

Jack and Elizabeth sprinted up the stairs and out the front door.

Gavin slowed the car to a stop in front of a warehouse in the downtown district.

"This is where he lives?" Gavin asked.

"Works," Manuel corrected.

The three men got out of the car and walked to the front door. A small security camera in the corner of the doorway locked in on them.

"Can I help you?" a voice came from the intercom.

"We are here to see Slider. It's Manuel."

A buzzer sounded and the front door clicked open.

Gavin pushed the door and Manuel walked inside as the other two followed.

*   *   *

Jack made a left onto Main Street and drove the speed limit looking out his window.

"We are never going to find them," he said.

"We will," Elizabeth said as she scanned her side of the street.

"Elizabeth, we don't even know where to look and if they are on their bikes then they know every little side road and short cut around this town."

"Isn't this your town, too? You should know the streets," Elizabeth said.

"It's been a long time," Jack said.

"Well, you better come up with something because time is running out."

"I know," he said. "I know."

The car moved forward as Jack and Elizabeth sat in silence not sure where to go or look next.

CHAPTER TWENTY-FOUR

Slider

The large room did not look inviting. The lights were dim and reminded Gavin of a Halloween haunted house. Four large television screens surrounded a console in the middle of the room. Multiple sonar and tracking systems were set up with grids of the city. No one was in the room.

Dillon, a bit nervous, put his hand on his revolver as he walked into the room.

"Sit down," a bold voice said, piercing the air.

Manuel, Gavin and Dillon sat on three chairs facing the computer console.

"To what do I owe the honor of this visit, Manuel?"

"Well, Slider, we have a problem," Manuel said toward the blank computer screen.

"Looks to me like *you* have the problem, not *we*."

"Yes," Manuel agreed. "I need someone to get a medallion back to me that was stolen. A teenage boy has it and my team here seems to have scared the boy and he is on the run."

"Boys do not run far," Slider said. "What about his parents?"

Gavin took that question, "I don't think he would go there. The father isn't really interested in him and the mother is afraid of her own shadow."

"Why call on me, Manuel?" Slider's electronic voice asked. "I mean a kid has brought you here? Kind of embarrassing isn't it?"

"That's true," Manuel said. "It is embarrassing, but you might be interested in this boy's extended family."

"It matters?" Slider mocked.

"When it's Jack Reed's nephew, yes it does," Manuel said.

"Diamond Jack Reed?" Slider asked, his voice showing much more interest.

"One and the same," Manuel said. "In fact he's here in town looking for his nephew as we speak."

There was a long silence causing Gavin and Dillon to shift in their seats uncomfortably.

"I don't think I need to tell you what happens if Jack finds the boy and the medallion first," Manuel said.

Gavin and Dillon leaned back in their chairs as a large figure appeared before them dressed in black, his hair short with dark unrevealing eyes.

"So nice of you to come out," Manuel said.

"Jack and I go way back," Slider said.

"I know," Manuel said. "Quite the rivalry wasn't it?"

"It was until he stole from me," Slider said. "All these years I have waited. I'm glad you brought this to my attention."

"Let's put our priorities in line," Manuel said. "First the medallion, then Jack Reed. But remember the medallion comes first."

"Okay then," Slider said. "It's obvious this kid, what is his name?"

"Tommy," Gavin said.

"Tommy has run to some friends for help. He's what, thirteen? Fourteen? His parents don't understand him. But all kids his age feel that way which is why he turns to his friends. If he has the medallion, where would he go once he got with the friends? Does he know what it can do?"

Dillon moved slightly in his chair and said, "He did disappear on us once."

"Disappear?" Slider asked, surprised.

"Yeah," Gavin said, "right in front of us just poof…gone."

"So suffice to say he knows that the medallion is magical," Slider said. "But finding information about the artifact will be hard and the material he does find will be sketchy because he won't know where to look."

Slider started to pace the room as he continued to think out loud. "Where could he find information about the medallion not readily available on the Internet or the…" he stopped pacing. "I know where he is."

"Where?" Manuel asked excitedly.

"The Exhibit of Mythological Artifacts."

"Why?" Dillon asked.

"It's the only place to go," Slider said. "It has been advertised in the local newspaper for weeks. The artifacts on display are from legends and folk tales. He will be looking for a replica of the medallion and the information that goes with it."

"Where is the exhibit?" Manuel asked.

"The Civic Center," Slider said, "but we are going to need more men."

"Not a problem," the rich man said.

"Then we go to the exhibit and wait for the kid to arrive," Slider said. "And if the famous Diamond Jack Reed should be there, too, we can kill two birds with one shot."

"You meant stone," Gavin corrected. "Two birds with one stone."

Slider gave Gavin an icy glare. "No, I meant what I said."

Gavin looked at Dillon and nodded, "Okay, we'll get the car."

Jack tried to enjoy his cheeseburger but his mind prevented it. Elizabeth ate a Caesar Salad which from Jack's view looked really healthy and something to be avoided.

"Food is good," Elizabeth said as she wiped her mouth.

"Best burgers in town," Jack said as he dipped a greasy soaked fry into some ketchup.

"We have been here for a half hour. You got any ideas about your nephew?"

"Not one," Jack said as he opened a local newspaper.

"Anything good in there?"

"Boring townie stuff," Jack said and spread the paper over the table to scan both pages.

That's when Elizabeth saw the ad. "Mythological Artifacts Exhibit at the Civic Center." The words went through Elizabeth's mind as Jack turned the page.

"I got it," she said.

"What?" Jack asked, surprised.

"Look," Elizabeth grabbed for the paper and turned to the advertisement and pointed.

Jack's eyes read quickly and he smiled. "That's it," he said, "let's go."

Jack threw a twenty dollar bill on the table and headed for the door with Elizabeth following.

"How far away is that Civic Center?" Elizabeth asked.

"We'll be there in fifteen minutes," Jack said.

Once in the car Gavin couldn't hold his tongue any longer. The idea of more men being involved in this mission upset him. He cherished his job and didn't like others telling him how to do it. It became even more important when money was involved.

"Boss you know that Dillon and I are perfectly capable of getting this kid," Gavin said. "I mean I understand about bringing in Slider but do we really need more men?"

Manuel had his phone to his ear. "If Slider thinks they are needed then we will do it," Manuel said. "You will not receive any less money, Gavin, so don't worry. Once the medallion is in my possession your money will come." The line picked up and Manuel said into his phone, "Yes, this is Manuel…thank you."

Manuel looked at Gavin and said, "You are still important to this." Gavin nodded but still felt angry about the entire situation.

"I am going to need a four man tracker team," Manuel said into his cell phone. "When? Immediately. I have already talked with Slider," there was short pause then Manuel smiled, "Good, *gracias*."

"Back to the motel?" Gavin asked.

"No, no," Manuel said. "The Civic Center, Gavin, the Civic Center."

CHAPTER TWENTY-FIVE

Running For Their Lives

The pedals moved fast while the Treasure Hunters Club swept down a hill through another suburban neighborhood. The one thing Tommy forgot when taking the back roads was all of the hills.

"How much farther?" Jackson asked as sweat dripped from his face.

"A ways," Tommy said.

"It feels like we've been out here forever," Shannon said.

"Longer," Chris said pedaling exhausted behind the group.

Part of the problem came from Tommy's insistence on hiding every time a car went past. Although it did allow the group time to rest, all of the stops made for a long trip and pushed the club's anxiety level to new heights.

"Tommy," Chris yelled, "I need a break."

Tommy slowed his bike and it skidded to a stop at a corner. He waited for the others to catch up.

"We just took a break," Tommy said.

Sweat poured down Chris's face and he gasped for breath. "I just need some water or something."

"We don't have time," Tommy said.

Shannon looked at Chris and said, "I could probably use some water."

"Me too," Jackson said. "Tommy it's not going to hurt our time or anything. We'll go to Lou's."

Tommy shook his head but agreed.

At a much slower pace the four bikes made their way around a bend and pulled onto the sidewalk of Lou's Convenience Store.

Lou Bagarenio ran his own store for over thirty years. He loved the location in a neighborhood where kids and families could walk to get whatever they needed. He was known for his homemade ice cream and his fresh baked bread.

Chris moved faster than he had all day. He dropped his bike, flung open the door and headed for the bottled water.

"You'd think he was a water buffalo," Tommy said.

"I think a water buffalo is tougher than Chris," Shannon said.

The others walked in and waved to the owner. Lou stood behind a counter wearing a dirty apron. For as messy as Lou looked his store was always emaculate.

"Chris, are you okay?" Shannon asked.

"Ahh," Chris said, holding the water after a prolonged drink. "This might be the greatest water I have ever tasted."

"What are you getting?" Jackson asked Shannon and Tommy.

"Fruit punch," Shannon said.

"Orange drink," Tommy said.

The three grabbed plastic bottles from the coolers and paid Lou for them. Chris paid for the bottle of water he drank and purchased another one for the road.

"Hot out there?" Lou asked grinning as he cleaned his hands on a checkered towel.

"Hi, Lou, yeah, a little bit," Tommy said and the rest nodded in agreement.

"Do you want anything else?" Lou asked.

"Are we getting any food?" Chris asked.

"I don't have any more money," Shannon said.

"Me neither," Jackson said.

Chris looked at Tommy who stared at the magazine rack in a trance. "Tommy?" Chris asked. "Tommy!" he yelled.

"What?" Tommy said surprised at Chris's tone of voice.

"Are you getting any food?"

"No," Tommy said. "Lou, can I use the bathroom?"

"Sure," Lou said. "Just turn off the light when you're done."

"I'll meet you guys out front," Tommy said and went to the back of the store.

"I think I have enough for one candy bar," Chris said scanning his remaining change.

Shannon and Jackson shook their heads.

After Chris bought his candy bar the three walked outside. A blue car pulled up and four men got out. They didn't speak but they grabbed the three youngsters and held them.

"Get the bikes," one of the larger men told another.

"Who are you?" Shannon asked.

"FBI," the man said.

*   *   *

Inside the bathroom Tommy washed his hands and walked through the store. He waved at Lou who was cutting roast beef.

"Tommy, have a good one," Lou said.

"Thanks, Lou, I'll see you later," Tommy said and pushed open the glass door and walked out.

Tommy didn't get two steps before he heard Shannon yell, "Run, Tommy, they're here!"

Tommy saw two men holding Shannon, Jackson and Chris and he bolted for the bikes. They were guarded. One large man held two bikes and another smaller man stood by the others as Tommy approached.

Tommy threw his hands out shoving the smaller man to the ground as one bike fell while Tommy grabbed the other.

Tommy jumped on, unsure if the bike was his, and started pedaling.

The larger man lunged at him but missed and landed on the ground. Tommy started up the road as the two goons followed on foot.

Tommy felt like he was riding in mud. I've got to go faster, he thought. He repeated it to himself over and over again, faster faster; I've got to go faster. In his pocket he felt the familiar burn from the medallion searing into his leg. He yelled out in pain.

Suddenly his feet were moving beyond himself. He was no longer pedaling on the ground but in the air. He was flying. The bike took off in a blaze of fire and smoke and left his two pursuers in the dust.

The two men stopped as Tommy disappeared between the tree tops.

"Call Slider," he said. "Tell him we've got the friends but lost the kid."

The smaller man flipped open his cell phone and hit a button.

*   *   *

Tommy's eyes bugged out of his face as he hung onto his bike, now a flying machine. By leaning left or right, he dipped and dropped his way around trees and power lines. When he finally landed the bike bounced several times on the pavement before Tommy slowed the bike to a riding speed. He stopped and breathed deeply.

How does this medallion do that, he wondered? He felt the heat leaving the blue jewel.

All of the answers were about a mile away. However, Tommy felt a strange feeling of emptiness. He'd have to continue alone. As a treasure hunter, Tommy knew going forward was the only way to solve the problem. And hopefully, he thought, by solving this problem he would free his friends.

Tommy pushed the pedal forward and rode the old fashioned way to the Civic Center.

*   *   *

Slider was not easily impressed and less so when men hired to do a job were tricked by a kid.

He did not express any anger to the four-man team over his cell phone. He did give them instructions on what to do next.

"Good work getting the friends," he said. "Having them out of the way will be helpful. Take them with you to the Civic Center and I'll take care of the rest."

Slider closed the phone, grabbed a gym bag, put on a black ball cap and headed for the door.

*   *   *

Manuel, Gavin and Dillon sat in the car eating tacos and waiting. Though he was not a man of patience, Manuel showed a remarkable ability to exercise the virtue when he wanted.

"What are we waiting for?" Dillon asked, his mouth full of food.

Manuel sat in the backseat of the Mercedes while Gavin and Dillon sat up front.

"Slider said the kid would show up here," Manuel said.

"How does he know?" Gavin said annoyed. "We are putting an awful lot of trust in this guy and money, sir, don't forget the money, for maybe a chance encounter. I find it hard to believe he's just going to walk across the..." Gavin stopped talking.

Dillon saw it too.

Gavin turned to his boss and said, "I'll be damned but there goes Tommy Reed riding his bike across the street."

Manuel looked out the car window and seethed, "Get him," he commanded. "Get him now!"

Gavin and Dillon leaped out of the car in pursuit of the young man.

CHAPTER TWENTY-SIX

Surprises Abound

Tommy put the bike in the rack. He ended up riding Jackson's bike and he didn't have the combination to his bike lock so he left it unchained. Tommy took a look at the tires and smiled. The rubber was really worn down. Tommy shook his head. Man, flying was fun, he thought. But it was time for business.

Tommy stood in the line for entrance inside the Mythological Artifacts Exhibit. He continuously looked over his shoulder trying to spot anything suspicious. As he told himself not to be nervous, his insides turned over and over.

Before entering the exhibit Tommy put his backpack on a conveyor belt for the contents to be scanned. Tommy walked through the metal detector setting it off.

A large security guard pulled him to the side.

"Empty your pockets please," he said and produced a plastic basket for Tommy to put his things.

Tommy dug deep into his pockets and felt for everything, including the medallion. He put his house key, money clip, gum, lint and the medallion in the basket. The guard used an electronic wand up and down Tommy's body and casually glanced in the basket.

"Here," the guard said and handed the basket back to him. Tommy grabbed the stuff and put it in his pockets.

"Interesting medallion," the guard said.

Tommy looked at the guard strangely, surprised the man noticed. "Yeah," Tommy said, "I made it at school."

"You know we have a display with those kinds of pieces over there," the guard pointed.

Tommy didn't want to be rude. "Thank you," he said and continued on. He tried to blend in with groups of people but none were headed in his direction. He finally latched onto a large family and walked with them as they approached the medallion display.

Tommy stared at the medallions all lined up in perfect rows on a blue felt blanket. He searched and compared until he found his and couldn't believe how accurate the replica looked, all the way down to the strange markings.

For a moment Tommy felt relaxed as he gazed at the fake medallions. He smiled to himself amazed at the all the trouble a small artifact caused.

As he shook his head Tommy glanced over his shoulder and his smile went away. Gavin and Dillon made their way through the crowd.

Tommy froze. What should I do? he thought. Run was a good idea, but to where?

As Gavin and Dillon drew closer Tommy placed the real medallion on the felt display and pocketed the replica.

"What did you just do?"

An older round lady, wearing a gypsy outfit, walked over to Tommy.

"Did you just take something?" she asked as she examined the display.

"No," Tommy said.

"Are you interested in these medallions? They have tremendous stories to tell."

"You're not kidding," Tommy said with a slight laugh.

Just as the lady began her speech Tommy scanned the crowd again but couldn't find Gavin or Dillon. Where were they?

"I'm sorry," Tommy said hastily to the woman, "I've got to go."

The woman frowned. "You can come back," she said.

Tommy saw an exit and started toward it but masses of people kept getting in his way. Finally an opening appeared and he went through, only to find Gavin and Dillon blocking his path.

Panicking Tommy turned to run and slammed into an older gentleman and fell to the floor. Tommy looked up and the man smiled at him.

"Careful el Chico," puffed the heavily accented words.

Tommy scrambled to his feet said a quick apology and started for a different exit. He noticed men in dark suits and sunglasses appearing at every turn.

Tommy moved through a group of kids and ran into the same elderly gentleman again.

The old man smiled and said, "I believe you have something we want."

Tommy looked at him confused. "What are you talking about? Who are you?"

"Tommy!" A familiar voice came through the crowd. "Tommy!"

The old man and Tommy turned and saw Jack with Elizabeth waving their arms at them.

"Get away from him," Jack yelled.

Tommy's eyes fixed on the old man who glared at the youngster. Tommy tried to run but Gavin and Dillon grabbed him before he could move.

"You're not going anywhere," Gavin said as Tommy struggled to break free from the iron grip.

"Get him out of here," Manuel said.

"What about those two?" Gavin asked.

"Not our concern," Manuel said and moved with Gavin, Dillon and Tommy to a nearby exit.

Jack and Elizabeth knocked over several people in an attempt to get to Tommy and Manuel as they saw them leave.

"The far exit Jack," Elizabeth yelled.

As Jack reached the door three men in dark suits tackled him to the ground. The treasure hunter bucked and rolled and got to his feet as the three men grabbed for him. Jack turned to the exit door when another man, seemingly from out of no where, jumped on him slamming him into the door.

A crowd began to gather as the melee continued. Parents tried to shield their kid's eyes as the fight smashed into exhibits and knocked over displays.

Elizabeth joined the fray and proceeded to kick her assailant in the stomach before landing a ferocious blow to the face. Elizabeth continued her assault on two other men who caught direct kicks in the stomach thrusting each man into a concrete wall and to the floor, unconsciousness.

Three Civic Center security men rushed in and tried to calm things, but Jack bullied his way through them.

"Come on," Jack said and he and Elizabeth ran to the side exit door. "It's locked, damn," Jack said.

"Front door," Elizabeth said.

The two ran toward the front of the building. Pushing open the glass doors they saw Manuel's car speed down the street.

"Where is our car?" Elizabeth asked.

"On the other side of the building," Jack said as the Benz disappeared.

"We were so close," Elizabeth said.

"Unfortunately," Jack said, "that isn't good enough."

*   *   *

Slider stood inside the front entrance and ignored the chaos around him. He opened his cell phone and punched in a number.

"Yes," Slider said. "I see them. You are in the clear. I will meet you back at the warehouse." Slider closed the phone and slipped it back in his pocket.

"I'll deal with you later, Jack," Slider said to himself and walked away smiling at the wreckage the small ruckus had caused.

CHAPTER TWENTY-SEVEN

Two Medallions

The damp smell from the warehouse caused Chris and Jackson to sneeze repeatedly and their eyes to water. Their allergies kicked in furiously and they couldn't stop their running noses. The group tried to loosen the ropes wrapped around their ankles and wrists but found the ropes too tight. Four large men in blue suits stood guard by them.

"Well at least we're on a real adventure," Chris said sniffing hard.

"This isn't what I had in mind," Tommy said.

"You said you saw your Uncle Jack?" Shannon asked.

"I did," Tommy said. "He was at the exhibit but Gavin and Dillon grabbed me first."

"Be quiet," one of the large men said. "You are not supposed to talk."

"Sorry," Jackson said.

One of the guards nudged the other and asked, "What are we waiting for?"

"Mr. Ernesto," the one replied.

Manuel emerged from behind a curtain wearing a black robe with red markings on each breast pocket and up and down the sleeves. He moved slowly, almost trying to show off the outfit for the group.

"Nice look," Shannon said.

"Yeah," Tommy said holding in a laugh. "Not many people can pull the whole warped, demented wanna-be, evil pope thing but you make it work."

Manuel smiled. "I'm sorry we were in such a rush at the exhibit that I didn't properly introduce myself. My name is Manuel de la Ernesto. And you are Tommy Reed, nephew of the famous Diamond Jack Reed."

"Yes," Tommy said, "you know him?"

"Of course," Manuel said. "As a matter of fact the reason you are in this predicament is because of him. If he had simply kept that medallion instead of sending it to you, things would be quite different."

"What makes the medallion so special?" Jackson asked.

"And you are?"

"Jackson Miller."

"Well, Jackson Miller, it is not one medallion that is special but when you put that one medallion with a certain other one, well," Manuel stopped as he realized how special the moment was to him, "it is something great."

"How do you know?" Tommy asked.

"Good question, Mr. Reed," Manuel said. "I see you have your uncle's inquisitiveness. The story goes back over 300 years to 1712 to be exact. In the Port Royal Harbor of Jamaica a terrible hurricane wiped out the port. At least 38 vessels were destroyed.

"During the storm a gypsy woman named Maria, who belonged to a secret society called the Leois, considered to be followers of the light, stole the medallion from a group called the Dorcha. The Dorcha, wanting peace, desperately needed the medallion and went after Maria."

"Who are the Dorcha?" Jackson whispered to Shannon.

"Followers of the dark," Shannon said. "I read about them in one of the reference books. But he's lying they were not for peace of any kind. They followed leaders of the dark. It said they are extinct."

"Silence when I speak!" Manuel yelled.

"I beg to differ," Jackson said out of the corner of his mouth.

"As I was saying, the Dorcha knew that whoever controlled the medallions would become all powerful and might possibly destroy the other."

"Then why didn't the gypsy woman just put the two medallions together and have the Leois destroy the Dorcha?" Shannon asked.

"Because she feared, as did her followers, that no group should be that powerful, not even her own. Pitiful woman. So she sacrificed herself and threw the Leois medallion into the Caribbean Sea."

"Which is how you got my uncle involved?" Tommy said matter-of-factly. "To dredge them up."

"He is the best, Tommy," Manuel said. "Now if you don't mind this talk has started to bore me and I do have so many things to do."

Manuel stepped away from his prisoners and took out his medallion and admired it for a moment. From his other pocket he pulled Tommy's. Just before he put them together he said, "Watch as I bring the powers of light and dark together to achieve ultimate power."

He placed one medallion on the other and slid them together so they linked. Shannon, Chris and Jackson closed their eyes. Tommy waited for Manuel's reaction. He noticed the guards take several steps back toward the exit door.

But nothing happened.

Manuel pulled the medallions apart and put them back together.

Again nothing happened.

Manuel looked at each medallion. Everything looked normal. He examined Tommy's closer and his eyes focused on some small print on the side of the medallion.

It read "Made in Taiwan."

Manuel exploded in anger.

"You switched them!" Manuel screamed and stormed toward Tommy. "You little," he swung with an open hand and slapped Tommy across the face. "Did you think I wouldn't notice?"

The slap stunned Tommy but he kept hearing his Uncle's voice in his head to hang on and keep fighting.

"The medallion isn't yours," Tommy said through clenched teeth.

Manuel glared at Tommy and breathed deeply, his anger slowly dissipating as he calmed himself.

"Did you put the real one in the exhibit?" Manuel asked.

Tommy didn't say anything.

Manuel nodded. "Your silence speaks volumes," he said and got within inches of Tommy's face. "Tonight you will get the real one back."

"In exchange for my friends' release, gladly," Tommy said.

"I was thinking more in terms of their lives," Manuel said, "and yours."

Before Tommy could respond he was interrupted by a new arrival.

"He's right you know," Slider said as he entered the room. "I do admire your moxy, young Tommy Reed, nephew of the great Diamond Jack Reed. Adventure must run in the genes, along with dishonesty and deception."

Tommy eyed Slider suspiciously. "How do you know my uncle?"

"Oh he and I go way back," Slider said and pulled a chair up closer to Tommy and the group. "So all of you want to be treasure hunters? Tough business, especially when people steal from you."

"Someone stole from you?" Chris asked.

"The great one did," Slider said smiling. "Diamond Jack himself came in and stole the cache which would have made me famous."

"I'm sure he didn't mean to," Shannon said.

Slider smiled. "Yes he did, dear. You see, men like Jack Reed have trouble losing and when I had him beat he had to steal."

"My uncle would never do that," Tommy said.

Slider shook his head. "You have misplaced trust, my dear boy. Do you really think Jack Reed is in the treasure hunting business for anything other than the money?"

"He's in it for the history," Tommy seethed.

"Is that what he told you?" Slider asked. "Then you are as dumb as I thought you were smart. Diamond Jack is about himself and no one else."

"Why do you really care?" Chris asked.

"Because tonight he and I will have a very fine reunion."

"He doesn't even know where we are," Tommy said.

"But he will or he isn't as good as I thought," Slider said.

Slider got up and walked over to Manuel. "Get the men in position. I will do what needs to be done when Jack arrives."

"What about the woman, Elizabeth?" Manuel asked.

"Two for the price of one," Slider said. "Not a problem." Slider turned back to the treasure hunters. "I am sorry that this is farewell but I am sure we will see each other again soon."

Slider picked up the large duffel bag and walked out the door.

*   *   *

Jack Reed stared at his beer and watched the foam fade. He hated losing. The uncomfortable feeling of defeat gnawed at him and his anger rose.

"The whole thing is my fault," Jack said. "If I hadn't sent him the stupid medallion we would have a ton of dough, my crew would be alive and Tommy would be out of danger."

"You didn't know that Manuel was such a bad guy," Elizabeth said as she sipped fruit juice and tried to cheer Jack up.

Jack shrugged and took a swig of beer.

Elizabeth felt sorry for Jack and that was new. He'd always been so sure of himself and now, she thought, she hardly recognized him.

"We'll find Tommy," Elizabeth said.

"Where? Do you have any ideas I haven't thought of?"

Elizabeth heard the frustration in Jack's voice. He never doubted himself, she thought. She always saw him as the great adventurer and for the first time Elizabeth saw Jack as human not a superman.

"Let's retrace our steps," Elizabeth said.

"Why?"

"Because maybe there is a clue we passed over or something we missed because of the fight."

"There sure did seem to be a lot of people helping Manuel," Jack said finishing his beer and ordering another.

"Maybe they were meant as a distraction?"

"Could be," Jack said, suddenly interested in the conversation. "Okay, walk me through."

Elizabeth put her drink down. "When we got to the Civic Center we saw Manuel and Tommy. They looked right at us but it seemed like we'd interrupted their conversation. They had to be discussing the medallion."

"So far you've stated the obvious."

"When we ran after them we went by the other exhibits and there was one about medallions."

"So?"

"What if Tommy saw Manuel's guys and switched the medallions?"

Jack leaned back in his chair deep in thought.

"No way," he said. "You're stretching it, Elizabeth. I mean even we didn't think of it. So I doubt Tommy did. He is a smart kid but not that smart."

"You said yourself he thinks well on his feet and what better place to make the switch. He knows its going to be guarded. Besides those fake FBI guys were the ones that grabbed him."

Jack's mind retraced everything quickly through his mind. Could Tommy have hidden the medallion in plain sight? It might be the best place, Jack figured.

"We've got to get back to that exhibit," Jack said.

"It's closed now," Elizabeth said.

"Doesn't matter," Jack said. "If Tommy did make the switch then Manuel is going to want it back tonight. We go now."

As he stepped in front of her, Elizabeth saw the old swagger in Jack's walk. He didn't like to lose, Elizabeth knew, and she liked that about him.

CHAPTER TWENTY-EIGHT

Return To the Civic Center

The car pulled up outside of the Civic Center just before midnight. Gavin and Manuel waited for the signal to proceed as Tommy, his hands bound, stared out the window. He couldn't help but think of his Uncle Jack and hoped he could find him.

A side door opened and a ray of light broke up the darkness.

"They're in," Gavin said. The large man pulled a knife and cut Tommy's ropes.

Manuel handed the fake medallion to Tommy. "We'll follow you in. Replace this one with the original."

Tommy got out of the car and started to walk toward the door.

"Don't think about taking off," Manuel said reading Tommy's mind. "If you do your friends will pay the ultimate price."

Tommy stopped and looked at Manuel who pointed across the street to a brown van. In the windows Tommy saw the faces of Jackson, Shannon and Chris. Knowing any move would be fruitless Tommy continued to the side door and walked inside, the door closing behind him.

One of Manuel's hulking men stood at the far end of the corridor and waved the group to continue.

As they walked Gavin whispered to Manuel, "Sir, why don't we just steal this thing?"

"Because according to the Dorcha code the current holder of the medallion must give it to another or the magic will not work."

"Even under duress?" Gavin asked.

"For the Dorcha that's even better," Manuel said with a smile.

Gavin nodded pretending to understand.

Three more men joined the group, the leader, a bald, heavy set individual, explained what his team had done.

"We did as you have asked, Mr. Ernesto. The security cameras are off and all silent laser security measures have also been eliminated."

"Good work," Manuel said.

Tommy stood by Manuel amazed at how large and a little frightening the exhibit looked with no people walking around.

"Go and replace the medallion," Manuel commanded.

Tommy hesitated and then started a slow walk toward the medallion display.

He replaced the fake with the original and held it tightly in his hands. He wished for invisibility hoping the magic would work but it didn't. He started to wish for another jelly incident but nothing happened.

As he started back to Manuel, Tommy felt he had to try one last attempt to save the medallion and his friends. He ran to the case that held Thor's hammer and knocked it over shattering the glass all over the floor as the famous mallet hit the ground with a loud clang. Tommy waited for the alarms but he only heard Manuel's laughter.

Manuel walked toward Tommy clapping his hands and smiling. "Well done, young man," he said. "You are quite the adversary, but did you really think I'd forget the security alarms on the displays?"

"I guess not," Tommy said disappointed.

"Now if you could be so kind as to hand over the medallion."

Tommy's hand loosened its grip on the medallion.

"Here," Tommy said and lowered his head feeling defeated.

"Everyone has to lose sometime," Manuel said.

"Not Uncle Jack," Tommy said almost whispering.

Manuel grinned, "Yes, even him. But you have provided much more excitement in this little adventure and for that I will reward you."

"How?"

"I will perform the ceremony in the hall with you and your friends in attendance," Manuel said proudly.

"Sounds terrific," Tommy said sarcastically.

"It will be," Manuel said. "Gavin, call Dillon and have him bring in the others. I don't want them to miss a thing. Now if you will excuse me, Tommy, I must prepare."

As Manuel walked away Tommy looked around the Civic Center. If Uncle Jack was going to show up he'd better make it fast, Tommy thought, it was about to get ugly.

*　　　*　　　*

In the upper balcony Slider got himself into position to view the entire floor area. He waited for the arrival of Diamond Jack Reed possibly with more anticipation than Tommy.

No matter what Manuel said, Slider knew that Jack would figure out about the switch and come after Tommy.

Slider fixed the scope on his high powered rifle and scanned the area reveling in the moment. He would end the treasure hunter's extraordinary career and with that reclaim his own.

CHAPTER TWENTY-NINE

A Diamond's Shine

On the hill overlooking the Civic Center Jack and Elizabeth watched as the rest of the Treasure Hunters Club were led into the building by a side door.

"We'll go in there," Jack said.

"I don't think they are just going to let us walk through," Elizabeth said.

"Force may be necessary," Jack said with a smile.

"I was afraid you were going to say that."

Jack and Elizabeth moved quietly through the darkness. The streets by the Civic Center were deserted with the exception of the occasional car. The street lights gave off a weak glow and allowed Jack and Elizabeth to approach the door undetected.

Jack turned the knob and was surprised to find it open.

Elizabeth's eyes widened, "Maybe we won't need violence," she said.

The words no sooner left her mouth when two suited men came storming down the long hallway.

Jack jumped at one, surprising him and the two crashed to the floor. The other raised his leg and slammed his heel into Jack's side. Jack winced in pain.

Jack kicked hard at the heel smasher's knee. The man grunted as his newly broken leg spun to the side. Jack pulled the other man to his feet and smashed him in the nose. Blood spurted everywhere, his nose broken. The man fell to the ground his hands grabbing his face.

Elizabeth gave three quick kicks to the other man and forced him to the ground. She landed six more kicks to the stomach and the last one to the groin, putting the man out.

Jack looked at Elizabeth in amazement.

"Good thing you didn't want to use violence," Jack said.

Elizabeth breathed deeply and said, "Yeah, good thing."

Jack smiled. "Use this," Jack pulled a rope from inside his leather coat and handed it to Elizabeth. "Tie them up and we'll put them outside."

*   *   *

Dillon led his three young prisoners through the exhibits and over to Tommy. Dillon waved to Gavin who nodded.

"Hey," Tommy said glumly to his friends.

They nodded not smiling.

"What's going on? Why are we here?" Shannon asked.

"He's got the two medallions and he wants to show us what happens when they are put together."

"What does happen?" Chris asked.

"Not sure," Tommy said. "But my guess is he's going to have some new power. Maybe he can just make himself invisible or something. I don't know but it isn't going to be good."

"That's comforting," Chris said.

"Stop talking," Dillon said. "Mr. Ernesto needs quiet."

Dillon walked over to stand by Gavin as they both waited for Manuel to reappear.

Moments later Manuel entered wearing the same black robe with red trim he had worn in the warehouse. He walked to the center of the great hall and stood.

"I have waited a long time for this," he began. "Three hundred years since that gypsy woman took away what rightfully belonged to the Dorcha. Now

I will avenge the dark warriors and combine the powers of light and dark for eternal and unwavering power."

"I don't know what is about to happen," Tommy said, "but I don't plan to watch it," and he slammed his eyes shut.

The others did not.

"I want to see this," Jackson said.

"Me too," Chris agreed. "Shannon?"

She didn't answer. The strongest member of the Treasure Hunters Club bit her bottom lip and trembled. Her eyes could not stop staring at Manuel.

Manuel gently locked the medallions together. He wrapped both his hands around them and closed his eyes. Thunder roared and lightening flashed as Manuel raised his hands in the air. Deafening screams rang out through the great hall causing everyone to wince and Chris and Jackson to shut their eyes as fear enveloped them like a blanket.

Manuel began to convulse and shake. He staggered and fell to his knees. The medallion shot red and blue lights across the Civic Center.

In one moment two beams came together and slammed into Manuel who screamed as the blast raised him off the floor and put him on the ground.

Then quiet.

Tommy opened his eyes and saw a horrifying sight. Manuel had been turned into an eight foot demon with red eyes and glowing finger tips.

Everyone in attendance could not believe what stood before them.

"I don't think that the power to become invisible is all he'll get," Shannon said.

"The power," Manuel said, "I can feel it pulsing through my body." He raised his boney and knarled hands in the air and fire shot from his fingertips shattering display boxes and statues. "The ultimate power," Manuel growled again.

He walked toward the youngsters and waved a finger at Dillon.

"Unbind them," he said.

Dillon and Gavin watched the entire event in a catatonic state.

"Now!" the demon screamed.

Dillon ran over and cut the kids loose. They rubbed their wrists trying to get feeling back in their hands.

"It is time for the four of you to be dealt with," Manuel said.

Manuel raised the locked medallions above his head and started to chant something in an unrecognizable language.

Terrified, Jackson did manage to say, "Any ideas?"

"No," Shannon said and she covered her head with her arms.

"My God," Chris said.

"Uncle Jack!" Tommy yelled.

Everyone including Manuel turned and saw Jack with the bow used by Diana, the Roman goddess of hunting, raised and ready.

Jack released two arrows and they struck Manuel in his clawed hand. The medallions fell to the ground as the demon screamed in pain.

"Get them!" Jack yelled and ran toward the medallions.

The medallions skidded across the floor as a mad scramble followed in pursuit.

Jack's hand reached out to grab the medallions but Gavin slammed into him and the two men slid across the floor. Dillon tried to get the medallions only to find Elizabeth's foot connecting to his face, knocking him backward.

Elizabeth lunged for the medallions but was sideswiped by a recovered Dillon forcing her to the ground.

"Get off!" Elizabeth yelled and kicked at Dillon who hung on for dear life.

Gavin, meanwhile, held Jack down and pummeled his face with punches. Jack got two quick shots in, eventually rolling over Gavin and gaining the advantage with six straight punches.

All four fought to exhaustion and stood facing one another, blood dripping in puddles on the waxed floor. Before either side could mount an attack the sound of a sinister and evil laugh echoed throughout the hall.

"Looking for this?" growled Manuel holding up the medallions.

"You've looked better, Manuel," Jack said as he and Elizabeth turned their attention to the large demon. "I mean I have heard of people letting themselves go but this is ridiculous."

"You are not looking all that good yourself," Manuel growled.

"I haven't been working out like I should," Jack said.

"Jack, you should have found this treasure and given it to me quietly. You would have had the money and no problems."

"True," Jack agreed.

"And that was all you were looking for, wasn't it? The big pay day. You didn't care about the treasure. It was for the money."

Tommy and the others looked on in disbelief. That couldn't be true, they all thought.

Jack looked at Tommy and the other treasure hunters he'd inspired and saw the pained looks on their faces. He'd let them down.

"There was a time when that happened, but it is in the past," Jack said. "Now hand over the two medallions."

"Sorry, Jack, but I have waited too long for this."

Jack stared at Manuel and looked deep into his red eyes. "You were there 300 years ago during that hurricane? You chased the woman into the harbor. That's how you knew where the medallion was and that there were two of them."

Manuel smiled and his large fangs dripped with saliva. "I was, Jack, and the gypsy woman thought she could hide them but she couldn't. She didn't know the power of the Dorcha. I waited patiently and now the power is mine."

"Not for long!" Tommy yelled and slammed into Manuel only to fall backward to the ground.

"You shouldn't have done that!" Manuel said and raised his large claw into the air and brought it down at Tommy.

Jack ran at Manuel. He crashed into the demon's chest but the impact knocked Jack to the floor.

Shannon, Jackson and Chris ran for Tommy and pushed him out of the way as the large demon claw hit the ground cracking the marble floor as the medallions slid away.

Tommy rolled to the medallions and grabbed them but the heat from their combined power sent a burning shockwave up his arm. Tommy immediately let go of the medallions and tried to cover his hand under his shirt to dull the pain but it didn't work. His hand already started to blister.

Manuel grabbed the rest of the club and threw them to the ground like rag dolls. The demon raised his large hand and leveled Elizabeth with one swipe. He walked slowly and stood over Jack.

"It's over, Jack," Manuel hissed.

"Tommy," Jack yelled. "No matter what happens, destroy the medallions."

Jack slipped away at the last second as Manuel's large claw smashed another deep hole into the floor. Jack could not get to his feet. Manuel continued his assault as Jack ducked and rolled away.

"Now, Tommy, do it!" Jack yelled. "Do it before it's too late!"

Tommy looked around for something to smash the medallions and spotted Thor's hammer. Without thinking he grabbed the famous mallet with two hands and raised it above his head swinging down on the medallions.

As the hammer connected the medallions shattered causing a massive explosion that sent everyone flying. In the balcony Slider was lifted off his feet and thrown back against the wall. Hundreds of blue and red streaks of light shot around the room each one lacing through Manuel who tried desperately to stand as he absorbed blow after blow forcing him to his knees.

The last of the beams slammed into his chest and he slumped to the ground, his body transformed from demon to a battered and burned old man.

Jack ran to Tommy. "Are you all right?" he asked helping his nephew to his feet.

"Yeah," Tommy said. "Where are the others?"

Tommy and Jack helped the rest of the Treasure Hunters Club and Elizabeth to their feet.

"Is everybody okay?" Jack asked.

They all nodded affirmative.

"Is it over?" Shannon asked.

Tommy turned and saw the moaning and crying Manuel de la Ernesto, a shell of what he once was. "I think so," he said.

"Good," Chris said. "Because I want to go home."

"Me too," Jackson added.

Elizabeth leaned on Jack and closed her eyes.

"Is she going to be all right?" Tommy asked.

"Just a few bumps and bruises," Jack said. "What do you say we get out of here and call the police?"

Elizabeth opened her cell phone and dialed 9-1-1.

"I'm glad that's over," Shannon said.

The first shot ricocheted off the ground causing everyone to look around.

"Was that a gun shot?" Tommy asked.

Three more blasts erupted and the group hit the ground scrambling behind anything for protection.

"Who is shooting at us?" Elizabeth screamed as shots continued.

Tommy remembered the man from the warehouse.

"Slider?" Tommy yelled out.

Jack's eyes narrowed, "Did you say 'Slider'?"

"Yes."

Elizabeth saw the look on Jack's face. "Jack, what is it?"

Jack acted as if he never heard a word she said. He looked around the exhibit and spotted what he needed.

"Stay here," Jack said to Elizabeth and Tommy, "I know who we are dealing with."

Jack looked up from behind his barricade and waited a moment before sprinting toward the display of David's famous slingshot and Achilles' shield. Jack grabbed the replica shield and hid behind it as he put the leather sling and rock in his pocket and made his way to the upper balcony. He pushed the heavy relic shield up one step at a time.

Slider reloaded and saw the moving target. He fired rapidly, shell casings hitting the floor with every squeeze of the trigger. Each shot bounced off the gleaming shield.

Another pause in the firing allowed Jack to pull David's famous sling shot from his pocket. Exactly like the one he used to defeat Goliath. Jack loaded the stone and waited. As soon as he saw Slider's head, Jack swung the sling above his head and let the rock fly.

The stone struck Slider just above his right eye, drawing blood and staggering him.

Slider found his footing and stood up for his nemesis to see.

"I've waited a long time for this, Jack."

"I know, Slider," Jack said. "I figured you'd be doing something like this now. How much is Manuel paying you?"

"It's not about the money," Slider said. "It's about revenge. You stole my life!"

"I did not," Jack said dismissing the comment. "You were never that good because the history meant nothing to you and you lacked patience."

Slider raised his rifle and peered through the scope, "I seem to have gotten over that." Slider's finger felt the trigger. "Say goodbye, Diamond Jack."

"No!" Elizabeth yelled and flung a boomerang at Slider. The wooden weapon spun in an arch and hit the barrel of the rifle throwing the shot off.

Before Slider could gather himself for another try he heard sirens in the distance. Slider quickly stuffed the gun in his duffle bag and headed for the rooftop exit. He did not look back at Diamond Jack Reed.

Slider entered the stairway and started up the four flights to the roof of the Civic Center.

There will be another time for Jack Reed, Slider promised himself.

Definitely another time.

CHAPTER THIRTY

Aftermath

Jack walked back to the others. He held the open sling dangling at his side and he wore a smile on his face.

"You guys can come out now," he said.

"Who was that?" Chris asked as he stood and dusted his cloths off.

"An old friend," Jack said.

"Do all your old friends shoot at you?" Shannon asked.

"Just the ones who don't turn into demons," Jack quipped.

Elizabeth limped over leaning heavily on Jackson's shoulder.

"Can you please explain that?" she asked.

"He was a treasure hunter a long time ago and he," Jack paused unsure of what to say about Slider, "he lost his way."

"So he tried to kill you?" Elizabeth said.

"Something like that," Jack said.

"I have known you a long time, Jack, and I know there is more to this than what you are telling me," his partner said.

"Elizabeth, trust me, it is not worth talking about," Jack said. "Where is Tommy?

Tommy stood by Manuel and knelt down next to him. Manuel remained curled up in a ball on the floor as tears streamed from his eyes.

"Are you all right?" Tommy asked.

Manuel started talking but his words made no sense and Tommy looked at the others for help. Jack and Elizabeth approached and saw what their former employer had become and a sad expression crept across their faces.

In the distance sirens wailed.

"Come on, Tommy," Jack said. "He's lost now."

"What's wrong with him?"

"The powers of light and dark are supposed to be separated. That way no one can abuse them. Manuel didn't see that," Jack said shaking his head. "He didn't realize that when the powers are combined it is too much for one person. No human can control all of that power. Not even a Dorcha."

"He seemed to," Shannon said.

"For a moment," Elizabeth sighed.

"He couldn't handle it?" Jackson asked.

"No one can," Jack said. "That's why the Leois put the power into two medallions and gave them to the gypsies to hide. They are meant to be apart."

"Thanks to Tommy no one is going to have that power again," Chris said.

"Thor's hammer really is the best," Tommy said with a smile.

"Tommy," Jack said, "I am very proud of you." He looked at the others, "All of you did a great job. You risked your lives to protect a friend and historical artifacts. As a treasure hunter that is always number one."

The main doors of the Civic Center burst open and a flood of policemen came through guns out and ready.

"Show your hands," Jack said. "Let's not give them a reason to shoot one of us."

"Don't move," a young officer said.

"We are unarmed," Jack said his hands in the air. "The people you want are in the exhibit and on the side of the building."

Several policemen rushed by the group and saw a beaten Gavin and Dillon unconscious and a hysterical and babbling Manuel.

Four policemen brought two other men in from a distant hallway and gathered them together.

"Who is responsible for all of this?" a large man in a tan trench coat asked.

"Go ahead Tommy, talk," Jack said.

"I guess I am, sir," Tommy said.

"I'm Detective Converse," he said. "Can you explain to me what happened here tonight?"

"Sure," Tommy said and started to recount the entire tale for the detective.

*   *   *

The stairs to the roof of the Civic Center made small, pinging noises as Slider scaled them. He pushed open the emergency exit door and jogged out on the tarred roof.

The numerous lights from the police cars lit up the neighborhood in blues and reds. He made his way to the far side of the building. With no other way out Slider jumped the 30 feet to the soft ground. He hit the grassy hill and rolled on impact.

His training allowed him to take the fall without serious injury. He limped his way through four alleyways to a parked BMW.

He got in the car, turned the ignition and drove away, his taillights disappearing into the darkness.

*   *   *

After 30 minutes Detective Converse stood in disbelief. "I've never heard anything like that in my life," the gritty policeman said

Suddenly an older gentleman burst through the front doors and Tommy and the other treasure hunters recognized him immediately.

"It's Mr. Thornberry, the director of the exhibit," Tommy said.

"Officer, oh my God, officer," Thornberry said as he saw the damage to the displays. "Who is responsible for this? I want them arrested and put in jail immediately. Is it these kids?"

"Sir," Converse said, "if you could just settle down a bit I can explain. I think."

Thornberry ran the Exhibit for Mythological Artifacts for over twenty years and never heard as wild a story as the one Converse told him about the medallions. No one believed Tommy.

Thornberry looked at Tommy and said, "There is no way that Thor's hammer was able to destroy anything much less gold medallions. It's a replica! They are all replicas."

"Well," Tommy shrugged, "it did."

"This is the most unbelievable story I have ever heard," Thornberry said shaking his head.

"Excuse me, Mr. Thornberry, my name is Jack Reed and I would be happy to help you replace some of the artifacts that were damaged or destroyed here this evening."

Thornberry eyed Jack and said, "You look familiar to me. Wait a second, are you *the* Diamond Jack Reed?"

"One and the same," Jack said smiling.

"I have read about you. It would be great honor to have someone of your expertise help with this exhibit. I think we should have a talk," Thornberry said.

"Sounds good," Jack said, shaking Thornberry's hand.

Jack flung his arm around Tommy's neck and he and the group walked out of the Civic Center.

CHAPTER THIRTY-ONE

A New Meeting

Chris and Jackson sat at the new rectangular oak table and couldn't help but smile.

Since the Treasure Hunters Club helped stop Manuel and his men, life had changed. Newspapers carried only the believable half of the story and it even got some national attention. People took notice of the group. Strangers from across the country sent donations to the Treasure Hunters Club.

The first thing to arrive at the clubhouse was five new computers to replace their old one. The group also received two laptops to help when they were traveling, not that the group traveled much. The club was also given new cell phones with Internet access.

Tommy, with Uncle Jack's help, purchased new equipment for their treasure hunts. Metal detectors, sonar equipment and new electro dialysis devices would aid the treasure hunters in the future.

The newspaper headlines "Teen Club Thwarts Crime" were under glass and hanging on the walls. Each article about the group was done in the same fashion and discussed each member of the Treasure Hunters Club and their role is stopping Manuel, described only as some kind of thief of ancient relics.

The group received an award from the donors of the Exhibit of Mythological Artifacts for saving the exhibit and increasing the interest level in the community and the rest of the country.

"It's been two weeks and I'm starting to miss all the action that went with the medallions," Chris said as he walked across the room and sat at a new computer.

"I'm not," Jackson said.

"Why?" Chris asked.

"We were almost killed by that demon, devil guy," Jackson said.

"But we weren't," Chris said. "Besides there is no such thing according to the reporters. Next time we'll be better."

"I don't know," Jackson said. "Why don't we just talk about lost treasure?"

"Because it's boring," Chris said.

They both turned their heads to the door when it opened.

Tommy walked in with Shannon and he carried a small box.

"What's in the box?" Jackson asked.

"The medallion," Tommy said and opened the box and pulled the medallion out.

"The medallion?" Jackson asked puzzled. "You destroyed it."

"I know," Tommy said. "Mr. Thornberry thought I would like a replica for the treasure shelf."

Tommy held the medallion up and admired its shine and beauty.

"Okay then," Chris said walking over to the group, "let's start the meeting."

Tommy sat at the front of the table and put the medallion in his pocket.

Chris asked, "What's our next adventure?"

"High school," Jackson said.

"Not that one," Chris said.

"Speaking of adventure, where is your Uncle Jack off to now?" Shannon asked.

"He said he's going to take some time off," Tommy said. "He felt really bad about the crew and how he was tricked by Manuel. He's just frustrated, I think."

"What's the deal with Manuel anyway?" Jackson asked.

"Last I heard he was moved to some insane hospital outside of Boston," Tommy said. "Detective Converse called and told me not to worry about him coming back."

"So what is our new adventure?" Chris asked again.

Tommy smiled. For all the times he wished he were out on the ocean or exploring some old mine shaft for treasure the thing he loved the most was his time with these people. Their adventures would come, he told himself, and they would be more rewarding because of each other.

"I say we head to the library and start with the new reference books," Tommy said.

"Good idea," Jackson said.

"I want an adventure," Chris demanded.

"No you don't," Shannon said. "Remember that 90 percent of all treasure hunting is research. So shut it, get on your bike, and let's go to the library."

"We can stop at Lou's," Tommy said. "I'll pay for cherry ice cones."

Chris shook his head and followed Shannon and Jackson out of the clubhouse door.

Tommy stood to leave and remembered the medallion in his pocket. He opened the new glass case for club artifacts and looked at the new materials, each one representing the club's adventure. Thor's hammer, given to the Treasure Hunters Club by Mr. Thornberry, sat in the center of the case. Tommy moved some buffalo coins, the TAB can, and laid the medallion against the back wall.

He smiled. What an adventure it had been, he thought. He saw the words "Made in Taiwan" inscribed on the side of the medallion and laughed. Tommy locked the glass case and walked out the door to join the others.

"I have great friends," Tommy Reed said softly to himself.

THE END

About the Author

Sean Paul McCartney (He's not related to the Beatle) was born in 1971. He graduated from Alfred University in upstate New York with a Bachelor's in Communications in 1993. From there he played two exciting seasons traveling around the world with the Washington Generals playing against the famous Harlem Globetrotters. In 1996 Sean earned his Master's in Education and embarked on a career as a teacher. He is employed by Plain Local Schools in Canton, OH. The first book of The Treasure Hunters Series is called Secrets of the Magical Medallions and introduces the four teens Tommy Reed, Jackson Miller, Shannon McDougal and Chris Henderson. The series is a cross between *The Hardy Boys* and *Indiana Jones* with a touch of *National Treasure*.

If you want to know more about Sean, visit his website at
http://www.sean-mccartney.com.

Information for Teachers

A complete Teacher's Guide detailing methods and ideas to include in your Reading curriculum is included on our website, http://www.treasurehuntersclubbook.com. This guide was written based on the new National Standards.

The Teacher's Guide contains:

- Pre-reading Activities
- Journal Writing Activities
- Creative Writing Activities
- Discussion and Review Questions

LaVergne, TN USA
21 October 2010

201693LV00004B/9/P